A Pinot Noir to Die For

by **Wayne Kerr**

A

Black  wann

Investigation

A Pinot Noir
To Die For

Wayne Kerr

A Black Swann Investigation

Canusa Books

CANUSA LLC
265 – 4035 S. Gellatly Rd
West Kelowna, BC Canada

www.waynekerrnovels.com

Publisher's Note: This is a work of fiction. Names, characters, places, and incidents are a product of the author's imagination. Locales and public names are sometimes used for atmospheric purposes. Any resemblance to actual people, living or dead, or to businesses, companies, events, institutions, or locales is completely coincidental.

Book design © 2013, BookDesignTemplates.com

Ordering Information: Special discounts are available on quantity purchases by corporations, associations, and others. For details, contact the publisher at the address above.

CANUSA Books — First Edition

ISBN 978-0-9904179-7-2

Printed in the United States of America.

For Marlene,

Thank you for sharing your life

with me. I would be lost without

your love and support.

Love, Wayne

A special thank you to Frances and Dick for

their enthusiasm and assistance.

<u>Books by Wayne Kerr:</u>

Monsters and Miracles (X + Y Files)

Kristin's Ghost (X + Y Files)

Escape From Area 51 (X + Y Files)

Dwelf (Guardians of the Realm)

Ric-A-Dam-Doo (The Snow Devils)

Dead Ringers (A Black Swann Investigation)

A Pinot Noir to Die For (A Black Swann Investigation)

Murder on the Okanagan Express (A Black Swann Investigation)

Praise for *the Black Swann Investigation series*:

"An absorbing probe of how an ex-cop framed in a professional manner becomes a PI with license to investigate anything and everyone. The evolution of justice and exoneration makes for a spirited puzzler that will delight readers looking for intriguing stories and absorbing twists and turns of detective work."
—**Diane Donovan, Senior Reviewer,** *Midwest Book Review*

"Kerr's style is gripping, his writing leaves you wanting more. The suspense, thrilling action, and characters come alive..."
—**Roy L Murry, author of** *The Three Wives of Don Quixote Smith*

PROLOGUE

October 25th, 2018

Ten days after the capture of TCK

Obviously, Roscoe Parmentor hadn't turned out to be the TransCanada Killer, but he was a bad man and we'd crossed paths.

Canada's newest celebrity, Constable Hannah Buckley, was in Vancouver doing a second Canada AM interview. The media couldn't get enough of the beautiful blonde beat cop that single handedly captured the now infamous TransCanada Killer. She'd promised me that after all the hoopla died down she and I would take care of Mr. Parmentor. I'd decided not to wait.

Before I'd become a Homicide Detective with the Toronto Police Department, I'd spent a year and a half in Vice. It had had its exciting moments, but mostly the job had been down right depressing. None of the women I'd met dreamt as a little girl of growing up and becoming a prostitute. Ninety-nine percent of them were high, frightened or devoid of hope. Few believed there was any way out for them. Many got into the profession out of desperation, others were coerced and some of them were forced. Slavery still exists. Human trafficking is a multi-billion dollar industry. I'd been genuinely surprised to find out how big the problem is right here in Canada. Most of these girls were smuggled into Canada, but some of them were homegrown.

I personally had never met a pimp I liked. Almost all of them were sadistic bullies. They're bad enough, but human traffickers were worse -- soulless psychopaths who treated women worse than animals. I believed Roscoe Parmentor fell into this category.

The Okanagan didn't have the resources or expertise to combat someone like him. Penticton's vice squad consisted of one cop. Kelowna had a department of two. I needed information and help. Canada's national police force, the Royal Canadian Mounted Police, kept a federal database. It was a good place to start. The file Hannah had given to me was pretty thin.

I still had one friend with the RCMP that might help me. While in vice I'd worked several cases with an impressive young RCMP officer. Jean Kirkwood was smart, driven and ambitious. We'd had a lot in common back then and we'd worked well together. Jean had come forward as a character witness at my trial and had visited me a handful of times in prison. Those visits and her regular letters had been bright spots in my dismal life back then.

"Could I speak to Staff Sergeant Jean Kirkwood, please?" I spoke into the telephone.

"I don't see a Staff Sergeant Jean Kirkwood listed," the courteous voice at Toronto's main office answered.

"I'm sorry, she would likely have another rank by now," I said, realizing that her life hadn't been frozen in time like mine had spending a decade behind bars. "It's been a few years since I've seen her."

"One moment please."

"She is no longer at this branch," the voice informed me. "Would you like me to transfer you to her present location?"

"Yes, thank you."

"Hold please."

The line went completely silent. After fifteen seconds I was silently berating myself for not asking which branch she was with before the call transferred. After fifteen more I was about to hang up and call the Toronto office again when I heard a click.

"Office of the Chief Superintendent," a chipper male voice filled the line. "How may I help you?"

"I'm sorry, I may have been transferred to the wrong department," I apologized, barely able to hide the annoyance I felt. "I'm trying to get hold of Jean Kirkwood."

"Chief Superintendent Kirkwood is tied up with meetings all afternoon," the voice informed me. "Is there anything I can help you with?"

"Would you please have her call Reggie Swann? My number..."

"Please hold, Ms. Swann," he said and there was a soft click.

"Why that little bugger," I whispered into the phone.

"Reggie?" Jean's excited voice boomed in my ear. "Is that really you, girl?"

"Jean, it's great to hear your voice," I answered. "I thought I'd been cut off."

"If Lawrence had cut you off, Girlfriend, I'd have fired his skinny white ass," Jean laughed. "I don't care how many words he can type per minute."

"Except for being a high and mighty mucky-muck sitting behind a desk all day," I chuckled, "It doesn't sound like you've changed at all. Congratulations, by the way. I'm so proud of you, Chief Superintendent Kirkwood. Why didn't you ever say anything?"

"Maybe I should have; I guess I didn't want to remind you what you were missing out here." Jean was hesitant for a second, then her boisterous personality returned. "Seems like prison didn't slow you down at all, Regina Swann. Just a few weeks out and you already bagged yourself a serial killer. If TPD hasn't already hired you back, you should come work with me."

"Constable Buckley caught TCK," I protested.

"I know what the papers reported," Jean's voice got serious. "Don't forget I've seen you in action, Reggie Swann."

"Okay, the next time we get together I'll tell you what really went down," I relented. "The reason for my call is that I was hoping you could pull some files on a dirt bag for me."

"Good old Reggie, right to the point," Jean said. "I'll see what I can do. What's the name?"

"Roscoe Parmentor."

There was silence on the other end of the phone for several seconds.

"Are you joking," Jean said. "Did someone put you up to this? Because it's not funny."

"No," I replied, confused by Jean's response.

"I've been after that bastard for years," she said. "Still am."

"I'm confused," I admitted. "A Chief Superintendent wouldn't still be working vice."

"No, not vice, Dear. I supervise the Human Trafficking National Coordination Center here in Ottawa."

"I didn't know," I told her.

"Parmentor has tampered with witnesses and killed a CI, though we couldn't prove it," Jean told me. "I've arrested him twice and both times he managed walk out of the courtroom without a prison sentence."

"He's operating here in the Okanagan," I said.

"We know, but we don't have any evidence to charge him with," Jean admitted. "His organization is tight -- no one will talk. I'd give my eye teeth to see that man behind bars."

"He's still on probation, isn't he?" I asked, leading her to the solution I was about to present.

"Wait, you're not suggesting..." Jean began.

"It worked for us before," I reminded her. We'd run a sting on a particularly violent pimp fifteen years earlier.

"It's too dangerous," Jean disputed. "We were young and stupid then."

We argued for several minutes before she agreed, providing she supplied a whole task force and personally come out to oversee the operation herself.

-S -S -S

Two days later, my old friend was across the hall in front of a bank of monitors watching my every move.

I honestly didn't recognize myself -- the face and body in the mirror screamed high-end escort. I had to admit that woman looked sexy as hell, but she definitely wasn't me. It had taken two hours for a professional make-up artist to make me look like that. Blonde wig, fake nails, false eyelashes and a pair of other mostly false things had all contributed toward making me look like someone else altogether. I preferred the more natural, girl-next-door look. But this job required me to both look the part of an escort and be unrecognizable.

"All dressed up and nowhere to go," I said both to myself and to Jean.

"Sound and video are four by four," her voice came through the earwig they'd also outfitted me with.

I walked back into the five hundred a night hotel suite and sat on the edge of the bed and waited. With some help, earlier that evening I'd poached two of Parmentor's high rolling clients, who were now in cuffs facing solicitation charges. According to his file, Parmentor wouldn't let an affront like this to his business stand. He'd either recruit me into his hooker harem or kill me. Eight large RCMP officers in the neighboring suites were ready to charge to my rescue in either case. Still, I had to admit to being nervous.

The knock at the door startled me, even though I'd been expecting it.

"Here we go," I whispered towards one of the dozen or so hidden cameras that Jean had her team plant in the room. I walked to the door and looked through the peep hole. It was one of the bell boys I'd seen earlier.

"What is it?" I asked through the door.

"Champagne, compliments of the hotel," he answered.

"How sweet." I took a deep breath and unlocked the door.

A large man with a flattened nose and cauliflower ear shoved the bell boy out of the way and rushed through the door. I screamed and jumped back. A woman and a man closely followed the big fellow into the room. I recognized Parmentor immediately.

"That's her," the woman confirmed.

"Go wait in the car," Parmentor commanded.

I cowered in the center of the large suite, where all the cameras could see me, while she left closing the door on her way out. Both men watched me carefully. I glanced at my purse sitting over on the mini-bar and inched toward it. Parmentor nodded toward it and immediately the big man retrieved it.

"Thank you." Parmentor sneered at me, his perfect teeth looked out of place on his crooked face. "You saved my girls some work tonight."

"Boss, I found this, but no money." The former boxer's voice sounded like gravel. He held up a compact 9mm automatic and dumped the rest of the purse's remains on the floor.

"Where's my money?" Parmentor said, stepping menacingly my way. I lifted my chin and held my ground. His hand lashed out and clamped onto my wrist. He dragged me to him until my face was inches from his. His sour breath smelled of whiskey. "Don't make this difficult."

"It's my money," I said, more defiantly than I felt. His hand squeezed tighter. "That hurts." I put my other hand over top of his. "Maybe we can work something out."

"You ain't got nothing I haven't seen a thousand times before, Sweetheart," he laughed condescendingly.

"We're coming in," Jean's worried voice informed me.

"Don't be so sure," I said, emphasizing 'don't' for Jean's benefit. I smiled, caressing the back of Parmentor's hand suggestively. His grip lightened just a little. I wrapped my fingers around two of his. "Have any of your girls ever done this, Baby?" I looked him in the eyes as I began to squeeze. My fingers tightened with all the strength that more than a million fingertip pullups had given them. The dark beady eyes bulged wide as one of his knuckles popped. I knew what was coming and managed to duck under the backhanded fist that raced towards my face. With my wrist freed, I dove back onto the bed and rolled off the far side.

"You just made a big mistake, Bitch." Parmentor stared at me, ignoring his broken finger like it hadn't happened.

I needed to make him angrier. "You like pain, Baby? Come over here and I'll break the other nine for you."

"Gimme the gun," he ordered his henchman, "and toss the room."

The big guy handed Parmentor the gun and started flipping over furniture. He'd definitely taken his boss's command literally.

"Tell me where the money is and just maybe I'll kill you quickly," Parmentor aimed the pistol at my head. "If you don't I'm going to take my sweet time with you." The gun and his eyes drifted down my body.

"I killed the last pimp that tried to take my money," I said, taunting him further.

A sadistic smile crossed his lips. He aimed the gun at my knee and squeezed the trigger.

"You missed," I taunted again, confident the loud bang had signaled the cavalry.

He raised the gun and pointed it at my oversized chest. He fired a second shot just as the suite door crashed open behind him.

"Freeze! Police!"

Parmentor swung around and fired four rapid rounds at the first cop through the door. The officer kept coming. "What the fuck?"

"Pull that trigger one more time and I'll put you down," the lead man stated, his large revolver pointed at Parmentor's face.

The henchman, about to throw a chair, thought better of it as the second man through the door took aim at him.

All eight Mounties filled the room impressively fast. The gun and the chair had been surrendered by the time Jean walked in.

"I know you." Parmentor struggled as two of the Mounties pinned his arms behind his back.

"Roscoe Parmentor you are under arrest for attempted murder and a weapon violation while under parole," Jean said.

"I've beaten your bullshit charges before."

"Third time's a charm," Jean told him.

"My lawyer will have me out in less than a day," Parmentor laughed, then he nodded at the gun laying on the floor. "Besides, that's not actually a weapon, if there aren't any live rounds in it."

"Can I tell him?" I asked, bounding around the bed, my bloodstream still teaming with adrenalin.

"It was your plan," Jean answered.

"The clip in that particular gun holds eleven rounds," I said, stepping right in front of him. "Only the first ten were blanks."

The eyes bulged again as he realized what that meant. "You won't live to testify."

"They don't need my testimony to put you away." I batted my very long eyelashes at him and pointed at a flashing red light in what looked a lot like the room's thermostat control. "The whole event was recorded on that and a dozen other cameras hidden all over this room."

His lips clamped shut. Furious, he tried to lunge at me. Strong arms held him back.

"Read them their rights," Jean told the nearest officer.

"Yes Ma'am."

My part was finished. My name would not show up in any reports. Jean was still logging evidence a couple of hours later when I finally left the Penticton RCMP station and headed home. We made plans to meet for lunch the next day.

"I appreciate the offer, Jean, really I do. A month ago I'd have jumped at it." We'd chosen to eat outside on the deck at Salty's. It was breezy but the sun shone brightly, keeping us warm. I looked out at the small whitecaps breaking across Lake

Okanagan. "I'm not going to rush into anything. I'm going to stay here in Penticton for a little while."

"I thought you were more of a big city girl," Jean pointed out.

"I used to think so, too."

"If you ever change your mind..." Jean smiled, then started to chuckle. "We do work pretty well together."

"Without a doubt," I confirmed.

"It feels so good being out from behind my desk for a change."

"I'm still getting used to being out anywhere," I replied. "Jean I never told you how much it meant that you never lost faith in me."

"We're sisters," she said.

I looked into her big brown eyes. We couldn't have looked or sounded more differently; we'd grown up in opposite ends of the country and yet I knew it was true. Inside we were exactly the same.

"Sisters," I repeated.

"Now Sis, I believe you promised to tell me the unofficial version of TCK's capture. How did you manage to find a serial killer that no one else was even looking for?"

"I was dating him."

"Shut your mouth..."

"I kid you not."

An hour and a half slipped by unimaginably fast. I finally got to hear about Jean's impressive rise through the ranks. We could have chatted for ten more hours, but Chief Superintendent Kirkwood had responsibilities and a plane to catch. We said reluctant good-byes and before she drove off in her rental we'd promised to do a better job of sharing our lives with each other.

CHAPTER 1

May 15, 2019

Nanaimo, British Columbia

Cold rain had been pelting the small city from early morning through to the evening and it did not appear to be letting up any time soon. The extra chill of Alaskan air that had pushed its way down the rugged British Columbia coast overnight added an unwelcomed notice that winter wasn't quite ready to yield to spring on the island. The wet, muddy conditions prevented Guy La Roque from finishing the final day of blasting at Castle Ridge, a new home development a few miles north of town. Carved into the side of a hill made mostly of granite, he'd been blasting for over two months. The lucrative contract would cover his meager expenses for more than a year.

La Roque had inherited three things from his late father: massive shoulders, a love of hockey and a knack for blowing things up. Four things, if you counted a weakness for rum. His father had been a munitions specialist in the Second World War and had used the skills honed during his service to open a business when he'd returned home to Quebec City. Married late in life, his old man had been forty-four when Guy had been born. Guy was the eldest of three children born in rapid succession, barely a year apart. His father had had a generally dour disposition, saying little and showing even less emotion. The exception being hockey. His old man would talk about hockey for hours with him. Though Marvin La Roque had never played himself, he had a coach's grasp of the game. The La Roque family had season tickets to the 'Nordiques', plus they'd never missed a televised away game. From an early age his father began to groom Guy to take over the family business. However, hockey easily trumped demolition and his father couldn't have been prouder when Guy left home to play on a Junior B team out west.

La Roque's once hulking father had been a shell of a man when he passed several years earlier. He'd complained incessantly that the Nordiques moving to Colorado was the worse thing that could have happened to him, but he'd been wrong. Losing Guy's mother had devastated his father. He never could have imagined his father as weak before then. His father never fully recovered from her death.

Guy unconsciously tapped his Stanley Cup ring on the steering wheel. His size and knowledge of the game had made him a very good hockey player. It was the speed and quickness of the elite players in the NHL that exposed his one flaw as a player. He worked hard but no amount of training made up for a lack of fast twitch muscles. More often than Guy cared to remember during his career, and he did remember each time, a quick winger would get the jump on him and he just couldn't catch them. 'Slow as La Roque' had been a favorite fan jeer wherever he played. These days, he laughed about it, often joking that ironically it had been the explosiveness of the players in the NHL that had forced him into the munitions business.

After hockey, he'd had a few other prospects. He'd made a pretty good living selling Porsches for two and a half years until the prospect of folding his large body into yet another 911 became too much to bear. Real Estate came next, but honestly, he didn't have the patience to work with people who didn't know what they wanted. In his opinion, the customer was not always right. Ultimately, he'd followed in his father's footsteps, though at the other end of the country and too late for his old man to see.

Well-worn tires skidded for a second on the wet pavement before grabbing as the rust-tinged pale-blue 1980 Toyota SR5 truck turned right onto Pine St. heading toward the steady traffic of working stiffs leaving the downtown core of Vancouver Island's second largest city. The tapping stopped as he gripped the steering wheel firmly with his left hand and leaned hard to his right. His large fist collided with the heater core housing with a metallic thwack.

"Come on you piece of shit," he admonished and smacked it again. This time the fan began to spin. An angry horn blast notified him that he'd begun to drift over the median line toward the oncoming vehicles. He bolted upright and corrected his course with a jerk of the wheel. The sudden movement caused his alcohol-soaked brain to swim for a couple seconds. The little truck bobbed back and forth barely staying inside the lane.

A second shorter honk from another car prompted a glance at the driver whose face was shielded by a fist holding an upright finger.

"Same to you buddy," he hollered, flipping the bird back at him. "No harm, no foul, eh." When he drank, his slight French accent got thicker. The only time he spoke his native language was when he called his sisters, which was not very often in the past few years.

La Roque steadied the ship and checked the rearview mirror for signs of cops. Nothing. He'd had several run-ins with the local constabularies and showing off his ring no longer garnered him any favors. He'd been drinking all day until he'd run out of rum a short time ago. He was on a quest to get to the Liquor

Store before it closed, lest he be forced to spend the evening drinking in a bar, which for some reason, one he couldn't put his finger on, often led to arguments and occasionally someone taking a swing at him. At one time, this would have met with swift and brutal retaliation. Not anymore. He'd made a promise and had been true to his word, despite many temptations.

La Roque made the left onto Fitzwilliam St and decided to listen to the radio. The radio was about the only thing that worked well in the poorly maintained vehicle. Adding a litre of oil when the 'check engine' light came on a few months back was in fact the extent of upkeep the truck had earned in the two and a half years of service to La Roque. He recognized the female artist's soulful voice and hummed along. After getting tired of talk radio he'd begun listening to jazz, he'd grown to enjoy its soothing melodies. He could no longer listen to Rock stations. Hadn't for a long time. Not since his daughter's death. Hearing a song, any song, by a certain popular rock band was too painful.

"That was Nikki Yanofsky, who is nominated for two Juno Awards this year," a silky-smooth baritone voice announced as the music faded away. "Speaking of the Juno Awards, Sarah McLachlan is being inducted into the Canadian Music Hall of Fame this year. The news delighted most Canadians, but not all. It angered fans of the band Aurora, who have been complaining for years that the group is being intentionally snubbed because of their irreverent lyrics."

The driver's spine stiffened, scarred knuckles turned white as the announcer continued.

"Aurora has sold more albums worldwide than Loverboy and April Wine combined, both of which are already in the Hall of Fame. Don't worry fellow Aurora-ites, they will get in there. It is just a matter of time. Maybe next year, Aurora. Speaking of next year, it's been some time since Aurora has performed live. However, rumors abound of a possible North American concert tour as early as next year. For all of you die-hard fans out there, that just can't wait, I have news. Last weekend I took a trip to Penticton to visit my nana. I know... Sweet, right? Anyhow, while I was there I toured the winery of Aurora's lead singer and the man who wrote their many hit songs, Milo Getz..."

La Roque reached toward the radio, but his hand stopped mid-air. The damage was already done.

"... The winery, which, by the way, has the same name as the group's best-selling album, Butterface, was gorgeous with a spectacular view of Lake Okanagan. If you ever get a chance to visit, check out the tasting room. It is filled with priceless Aurora memorabilia, including gold records, guitars and hundreds of never-before-seen photos. Of course, there is also great tasting wine. Best of all, while I was there, the man himself, made an appearance and sang half a dozen songs. Which I'm told by the locals, he is prone to do from time to time. I had a chance to speak with the rock icon and here was his response when I asked Milo about the 'Hall of Fame' announcement.

"I love Sarah," Milo's distinct voice began. "She is a fantastic artist, a wonderful person and a very deserving recipient of the honor."

The brain-numbing buzz La Roque had spent the afternoon creating abruptly vanished at the sound of the singer's voice. The Toyota pulled off to the side of the road and stopped sharply as the front wheel scraped angrily against the high curb. An anguished guttural moan erupted from deep inside the man. His shoulders began to quake. His head sunk forward until it was resting on the top of the steering wheel. Tears fell freely onto his mud-stained jeans.

"Here at 101.6 Smooth Radio we love Sarah McLachlin, too," The announcer said as familiar music came up in the background. "For your listening pleasure, here is the lady herself."

"Adia, I do believe I've failed you. Adia I know I've let you down," Sarah McLachlin's haunting voice filled the cab of the small truck.

He lifted his hips, pulled out his wallet and flipped it open. Through his tears the smiling face of a teenaged girl with a mouthful of braces greeted him. He gritted his teeth, knowing that the smile had been a lie. For the millionth time he berated himself for being away so much. So focused on himself that he hadn't seen the pain she felt. Hockey, hockey, hockey… An enforcer who spent most of his career playing for farm teams, occasionally pulled up to the show to add muscle during the playoffs. He couldn't help thinking of spring 2008, when he'd been called up to play twenty games in the regular season by the Senators. It had been the happiest time of his life. He'd been too self-absorbed to see that his daughter was already suffering. The bullying had started. 'Two-bagger, Butterface', kids could be so cruel. Beatrice was beautiful to him, but she'd inherited his course features. Beatrice looked a lot like his sister, who'd eventually turned into a handsome woman.

May 24th, 1999, after being picked up by the Red Wings, he'd scored his first and only playoff goal, an overtime game winner on top of that. No more farm teams for him. His agent had been so excited. The greatest day of his life ended up also being the worst. Just before midnight amidst the backslaps and beers, his phone rang. It was home. He'd been expecting their call. They'd be so proud and excited. The gut-wrenching anguish in his wife's voice was seared into his memory. The celebration stopped, the world forever altered, life as he knew it was over. His twenty-four hour a day obsession with hockey ended at that moment. He hadn't laced on a pair of skates since.

"I spent more time sitting in penalty boxes than I spent with my own daughter. Fucking idiot," he hissed at himself, and pounded the dash, then slid his hand down and switched off the radio. Beatrice had been a Daddy's girl, up until her last few months. Normally, when he was home they'd been inseparable, however, she'd begun to spend more and more of her time in her room. He and Nicole had been concerned, but friends with teens had assured them it was normal behavior. They'd all been wrong.

La Roque missed his wife as much as his daughter. He'd known her all his life. Nicole had been his best friend's very pretty, older sister. He'd had a crush on her since first grade, that had only grown stronger as he got older. Somehow, in the seventh grade, she'd figured out how he felt about her and she'd teased the gawky teen mercilessly all through junior high. In high school the teasing turned into flirting and the flirting turned into love. By his graduation they were deeply in love. Nicky had held off going away to university. Instead, she went with him to Saskatoon, where he played a season for the 'Blades'. Nicky married him a year later. From first crush until this day, she was the only woman he'd ever loved, likely ever would. Counseling hadn't saved their marriage. In truth, they'd been a constant reminder to each other that neither had protected the most precious thing in their lives.

'Two-bagger', had been Aurora's biggest hit song and his daughter's nickname. If only he'd known.

"What would you have done?" he shouted at himself. "Beaten the shit out of every boy in the high school that had ever teased her, that's what."

"Girls, too?" his wife's voice echoed in his mind. He and his wife had learned that some of the girls had been even worse, sneaking up behind her in the school halls and jamming a paper bag over her head.

What could he have done? This debate had run through his head thousands of times. It usually ended the same way. He hung his head. Shame enveloped him.

He'd been no better. In high school, he'd given Jason Tremblay the nickname: Warts, after rubbing the nerdy boy's face into the frog he was about to dissect. His friends had found it hilarious. It had just been a stupid prank, but the nickname had stuck. Everyone called Jason 'Warts' after that day. Well, truth be told it wasn't everyone. Mostly it had been the jocks, like himself, who'd picked on the smaller kid and wouldn't let the nickname die. He'd known Jason didn't like it but hadn't cared. It was just harmless fun, right?

A few years later, enlightened about the social and psychological effects of bullying after his daughter's death he'd sought out Jason Tremblay. Unlike his daughter, Jason had survived high school. He'd become a very successful businessman. The man had graciously accepted his apology, but Guy knew that a confession and an autographed jersey could never make up for the grief he'd caused the boy.

If only Beatrice had told him or his wife what she was going through...

It was that song! That goddamned song! 'Two Bagger' puts Milo Getz into the hall of fame and my only child into the ground.

"It's not fair, damn it!" He kissed his daughter's face and tucked his wallet away. That damned song had taken both Beatrice and Nicky from him, while it had made Milo Getz rich and famous. "You have your very own winery, how fucking nice for you."

As La Roque slid his hand from the steering wheel toward the gear shift, he spotted a box of blasting caps sitting on the passenger side floor. His breathing stopped. His hand hovered motionless above the worn five-speed stick shift as evil intent pushed aside the desire for a tall glass of Bacardi with a splash of Coke.

"Milo, I think I will drop in for a tasting."

His adrenalin surged as La Roque felt an actual sense of purpose for the first time since that night almost two decades earlier. He wiped the remaining tears from his eyes. They were replaced by fierce determination. Come rain or shine he'd finish the Castle Ridge job tomorrow. He now had more important things to attend to. The little truck pulled forward and then with the slightest break in traffic pulled a u-turn in the middle of the street, eliciting a chorus of horn blowing. La Roque didn't notice, his mind was already planning a visit to a particular winery in the Okanagan.

CHAPTER 2

May 21, 2019

Penticton, British Columbia

"**D**on't do it," I whispered, watching Barb Longwell get out of her ten-year-old Corolla near the Ogopogo Motel. I hadn't started Black Swan Investigations to find out who was cheating on whom. Though, what did I really expect would happen? There wasn't much international intrigue in the Okanagan. I'd already helped capture a serial killer and shut down a prostitution ring. Nothing that interesting was likely to happen in the region for another hundred years. Would it be too much to ask for a mysterious murder or kidnapping to solve? A girl can dream...

I reluctantly snapped a couple of pictures as Barb stepped onto the property. It looked like her husband, Brian, had been right about her having an affair. I'd known both Barb and Brian since elementary school. They'd been high school sweethearts.

Everybody liked them. Barb and Brian, Brian and Barb -- they were a matched set. I could not imagine them separately. I might have to start.

Brian had become suspicious after coming home from work one night, an hour earlier than usual, and his wife wasn't home. She'd arrived thirty minutes later, claiming to have been out to a late movie with a friend. The thing about Barb, he'd told me, was she never lied to him. It turns out she wasn't very good at it. Her eyes gave her away. They'd had a few bad breaks and were going through a rough patch, but he never thought Barb would do something like this to him or their family. He needed to know.

Brian, like every other person in the country -- at least it seemed that way to me, had followed my continuing saga in the paper and on the news. My life had been juicy watercooler gossip: homicide detective murdered police psychologist to avoid suspension from duty; the 'Black Swann', as the press had dubbed me, was sentenced to life without the possibility of parole; finally freed from prison after ten extremely long years, when damning evidence and testimony from original trial was deemed false and/or inadmissible; the Toronto Chief of Police still believed I was guilty and vowed to prove it; former cop (me) helped Penticton police capture a serial killer (incredibly the same man who'd framed me); new Toronto PD Chief apologized for predecessor and offered the fully-exonerated former homicide detective(me again) her old job back; I'd declined and instead opened Black Swann Investigations in Penticton. My highlight reel wasn't pretty.

Despite capturing the real murderer, I knew that many people would harbor doubts about me. After spending eight years in federal prison most cops would never look at me the same. I didn't blame them. Hell, I didn't view myself the same. Prison changes a person. I had the stink of prison time surrounding me, I probably always would. A good cop can spot it, I always could. During my incarceration, I'd lost the career I'd worked very hard to develop. I'd also lost my home, my husband, nearly my life several times and discovered how few true friends I'd actually had in Toronto. When all had been said and done, I'd decided to stay in the town I'd grown up in. A place where there were some people I could count on and others who actually gave me the benefit of their doubt. I had friends and family here, helping me rebuild my life. The one person who'd never given up on me, even after I had, lived here – my mom. Without her, I'd still be rotting away in prison or worse.

Brian had also read the papers and knew I'd started a Private Investigation business and came to see me. I'd told him that I didn't like these kinds of cases, but he'd insisted. The Longwells weren't rolling in dough and I'd ended up giving him the friends and family discount. I seemed to be doing that for a lot of my clients. Luckily for Brian, I was barely two hours into Barb's surveillance and things were already happening.

I got off Betsy, my shiny red Vespa, stowed my helmet, then positioned myself across the street from the quaint little motel. I kneeled down behind some bushes and lifted my camera into position.

It had been an adjustment, getting used to the idea that I wasn't a cop anymore. There were a million things I liked about being a private detective: setting my own hours, investigating the way I saw fit, answering to no one, taking the cases I wanted, for the most part. However this was absolutely the worst part of being a PI in a small center. It seemed as though you knew almost everyone and their personal business. It was hard to say no to friends of the family, and my mom, from what I could tell, was apparently friends with everyone in the Okanagan.

"Turn around, Barb," I pleaded silently. "You've got two kids. What are you doing?"

This was my own fault, I realized. I'd rather be doing anything than taking these pending pictures. I could still have been signing books with Hannah in St. Johns or Fredericton, wherever she was today. But no, I was anxious to get back to Penticton and my 'normal' life. Even chasing down a skip-trace would be better than this. Oh yeah, I did that yesterday. Unlike his brother Darren, Doug Gordon had been easy to catch. I'd discovered that he was a huge hockey fan. He loved the Oilers. Fortunately, I hadn't had to make the long trek to Edmonton. Tuesday night I tracked Doug to a Vee's hockey game. His nephew was on the team. I'd nabbed him in the parking lot. When I'd gotten to work this morning, there was message on my machine. It was a case of the cheating spouse variety. This case.

Barb went directly to the Ogopogo office. Brian's wife and the young man at the check-in desk shared a laugh as she approached him. He got up from his chair and then Barb went around the counter towards him.

I readied my camera for the money shot. Seeing your spouse sharing a passionate kiss with someone else is often more devastating than any explicit compromising photos. The kiss was all I'd need. My finger pressed down as they neared each other.

"What the..?"

I managed ten or eleven rapid-fire shots of Barb slipping past the young man and taking his place behind the check-in counter before my finger let up. I watched as he pointed to something on the nearby computer screen. Barb nodded. Their interaction appeared professional and completely plutonic.

"Barb Longwell is not a cheater," I said, doing a small but adamant fist pump with my free hand. I then zoomed in even tighter and snapped a couple pictures of her typing on the computer. Probably logging in, I guessed. Team Barb and Brian were alive and well. This thought made me smile. Kneeling behind the bushes, I chuckled as I dismissed an idea for a slogan on the website Hannah and Erika were building for me: I'll get down on my knees to give you a happy ending. They would get a kick out of that one, especially Hannah. My friends had convinced me that I needed an online presence in today's world. After much resistance to the idea, I'd reluctantly agreed, but drew the line at social media. FaceBook, Twitter, Pinterest and all the rest of them had happened while I was away. I didn't get it. Maybe, it's because my life has had so much media coverage already. My 'trials and tribulations' Alan had cleverly joked during our first date. So far, I've had zero desire to publicly share my thoughts and life with others. Privately on occasion, but publicly no.

Wait a second...

I lowered the camera as it suddenly occurred to me that this might not be such a happy ending, after all.

"Why doesn't Brian know about this?" I asked myself, aloud. Perhaps she's saving up to get her own place. Maybe she's paying off a gambling debt? Thoughts like these rolled around in my mind.

I checked my watch as an older Monte Carlo pulled into the parking lot and rolled right up to the office door, its tires crunching on stones as the big car came to a stop. Four o'clock -- a shift change, perhaps. The driver's door opened and a very pregnant young woman slowly climbed out. She waved at whom I assumed was the father of her baby, and Barb through the motel window as she waddled around to the passenger side of the car. Barb waved, while the young man grabbed his jacket and rushed outside.

For no good reason, other than it made me happy, I snapped a string of pictures as the young lovers kissed, just before he helped her settle back into the car.

I ducked down as they drove past, then took several more pictures of Barb working behind the counter. I was thrilled that Barb was not cheating. But, Barb had a job that Brian didn't know about. Why? Most of the reasons I'd thought of weren't good. Shame on me, if anyone should hold out for proof before jumping to conclusions it's me. However, in my defense, Barb was keeping a secret and I usually witness the wrong type of happy endings in these kinds of cases. I really wanted this not to be one of them. I stood and brushed the dust from my slacks.

I got back on Betsy and rode up to the Ogopogo office.

"Welcome to the Ogopogo," Barb cheerfully greeted me as I stepped through the door. "Checking in?"

Up close, I noted the stress lines on her face and the puffy bags under her eyes. If I hadn't already known her age, I'd have guessed almost ten years older. I hadn't seen her in person since just after high school, and though the cuteness of youth had faded, Barb was still better-than-average looking. Shortly after puberty struck she'd been blessed, or cursed, depending on how you looked at it, with sweater tugging boobs. Tonight, they were understated under a loose-fitting buttoned-up cotton blouse.

"No, I just wanted to get your rates for Thanksgiving weekend," I answered, fibbing big time.

"Certainly. How many people in the party?" Barb questioned me, as her attention and fingers moved toward the computer.

"Two couples, two rooms, for five days." I made up the details. "Wait, you're Barb Longwell aren't you?"

"Yes," she replied. Her eyes searched mine for a few seconds. I realized I was still wearing my helmet and tugged it off. That helped. Recognition swept across her face. "Reggie? Oh my God, it's been forever."

"Gotta be at least nineteen years," I said. I'd already done the calculations after speaking with Brian.

"I was so happy to hear that you got your name cleared from that whole mess out east," she said, as though things that happened in eastern Canada didn't really count here in the west. An attitude that more than one Prime Minister has harbored regarding Western Canada.

"Thanks," I answered. This subject often led to awkward conversations about my life in prison. The truth was more than most wanted to hear and difficult for some to comprehend. I wasn't very good at sugar-coating it. I'd found that it was better to skip past these types of questions as quickly as possible. "I'm just happy that the real killer is in prison instead of me and I'm back home in Penticton."

"I can only imagine," Barb said, with more depth than I expected. Her brown eyes were deep and soulful.

"I had no idea that you worked here," I said, quickly changing the subject.

14

"It's just part-time," Barb replied.

"Been here long?" I asked, to keep the info flowing.

"A few months," she told me, as she poked the computer keys. Just when I thought it would be a challenge to get her talking about her job, she began on her own. "Brian, my husband -- do you remember him, Reggie?"

I tilted my head as if I hadn't just spoken with him that morning. "Yes, I remember Brian."

"Well, he got laid off a while back and had to take a shift job over in Kelowna," she told me, without looking up from the screen. "Things have been tight lately. We'd burned through a big chunk of our savings while Brian was off work -- you know how it is. My boys are both teenagers now, and I hardly see them anymore, what with hockey and girlfriends and homework. I was getting bored and lonely in the evenings, then I heard the motel was looking for someone for four hours, three evenings a week. It seemed like a perfect fit. I'm saving up for a family trip this summer. For years Brian and the boys have talked about hiking through the Grand Canyon. I'm not looking forward to tents and sleeping bags so much anymore, but I know my boys will love it."

"That would be wonderful," I assured her. "An adventure they'd remember for the rest of their lives."

"I think so." She looked up at me and smiled. "Before we know it, the boys will be off to university."

"The years can fly by," I acknowledged the quick passage of time on this side of the prison walls. I heard the familiar sound of a printer spewing out paper. Barb rolled her chair to the side and reached under the counter. Her hand came out with two sheets of paper bearing the cute Ogopogo logo.

"Be sure to request rooms one through six, when you book," she informed, handing me the quote. "We just put new beds and flat screens in those ones."

I thanked Barb for her help and promised to drop by her house one morning to catch up.

"Thank you, Mrs. Longwell," I said again, this time to myself, as I pulled on my helmet. I was still smiling as I rode out of the motel lot. I'd followed her here expecting to witness betrayal and I got just the opposite. Tonight felt like a victory. My faith in human nature restored. I felt good. I decided to celebrate with an apple fritter and hot chocolate, something I'd done ever since I was a teenager. Besides my mom and dad, my ex-husband Trent and freedom, I'd missed apple fritters the most. Though, honestly, besides daily survival, there had been nothing worth celebrating during my ten years of incarceration. Perhaps, that is really what I'd missed about fritters.

The Tim Horton's on Fairview wasn't busy. I carried the sweet bounty to my usual table. I told myself I'd chosen this spot because the duct above delivered hot air when it was cool outside and air-conditioning during the summer months. The truth was, I sat with my back to the corner. I could see the entire place from here and no one could get behind me -- a remnant from my prison days. An ex-cop had no friends in prison. I still could not relax in a crowd, especially if people were milling around behind me.

I was lucky to have such understanding friends as Hannah, Erika and Rhonda. I pretty much had to sit in the worst seats in the house when we went to a movie, concert or hockey game. If my back wasn't up against the rear wall, I couldn't concentrate. Though I'd protested, they always insist on sitting with me.

Time does fly by on this side of the concrete and razor wire. It was hard for me to believe that I'd been out of prison for eight, no wait... I counted on my fingers to be certain, wow, nine months already. It seemed like only a few days ago Erika White took a chance and hired an ex-con to do some investigating for her firm, White Garrison and White. Capturing the Trans-Canada Killer (TCK), hadn't only saved Hannah's job, she'd been promoted and was now a homicide detective at the Penticton Police Department. White Garrison and White was busier than ever. Rhonda, Erika's assistant, now had an assistant of her own and Erika was doing lots of trial work which makes her happy. I'd hung my shingle, in the form of gold lettering, right underneath the White Garrison and White sign. Her father finally retired and Erika insisted I take his office. It was a little stodgy and the faint cigar odor persisted, but there were French doors leading out to the back yard so I could come and go as I pleased. At first I thought I'd redecorate, but the dark wood-panel décor was growing on me. I had turned the large desk around and slid it back a few feet. It made the place seem roomier, plus I could see both doors from my chair and make a hasty exit out either one, if necessary.

The receptionist, Mrs. Litmus, still acts as though I'd wandered into the wrong building every time I step through the front door. I dress too casually for her taste. I'd win her over eventually.

Like most cops, I'd despised private investigators. I'd never dreamed for a second that I'd ever be one. Now I couldn't imagine being anything else.

I polished off the last of the lukewarm hot chocolate and headed for home.

CHAPTER 3

Hannah returned from the eastern seaboard Thursday evening and called as soon as she hit the tarmac. She excitedly filled me in on our rapidly rising book sales. Hannah had a wonderful time in Montreal and the Maritimes. She and Jennifer, our publishing rep, had hit it off immediately. I knew they would after spending several days with the sparkly young woman during my portion of the book tour.

"It really is a half hour later in Newfoundland," Hannah laughed. "Those east coasters put us west coast pansies to shame in the drinking department, I can tell you."

"That I already knew," I replied, remembering the law enforcement conference I'd attended in St. Johns many years earlier.

"I'm going to crawl right into bed as soon as I get home," Hannah announced.

"Flying from one coast to the other is no fun," I said, "You must be tired."

"I didn't say that," she laughed. "I haven't seen my man in over a week..."

"TMI," I cut her off.

"Just kidding," she said, stifling a yawn. "Excuse me."

"You really enjoyed the book tour?"

"Oh, my God, yes," Hannah exclaimed. "Though, I'd take Danny along on the next one. Of course, we'll need another mysterious murder or kidnapping to solve for that to happen."

"You don't mean that?" I asked, as though I hadn't been wishing for a juicy case myself.

"I don't?" she teased. "Room service definitely beats cooking, I'm just saying."

"I did enjoy the room service," I conceded.

For the next few minutes we joked back and forth about how unlikely it would be for another murder to happen in sleepy Penticton. We had no idea just how soon we'd be seeing a dead body.

"There's Danny," Hannah's voice became excited. "My ride is here."

"You are talking about a car ride?" I blurted out, shocking both of us.

"Reggie, I'm surprised at you!" Hannah jokingly admonished. "There's a naughty side to you, after all."

"I'm the Black Swann, remember?" I laughed. "Run tomorrow?" I asked, hoping to jump back into our routine, of Mondays, Wednesdays and Fridays right away.

"See you in the morning. Gotta go. Bye Reggie."

"Bye," I quickly added. Then just before the line went dead I heard Danny's voice, "Baby, have I missed you." I pictured her throwing her arms around her husband and smiled. Then, because I'm an idiot, I thought about being in Trent's arms. I shook my head. Trent is gone, I told myself for probably the twelve hundredth time. Brain and heart don't operate at the same speed. Even though we'd been divorced for seven years, resuming my marriage had been a large part of the 'getting my old life back' fantasy I'd clung to in prison. Trent, our house, my job and the kids we were going to have, made up the world I loved to disappear into once my cell door locked at night. Sometimes, I'd also imagine that my father was still alive. Dad had gotten along so well with Trent, that a casual observer might have thought he was the son and I was the in-law. I didn't mind, in fact, I was thrilled. We were all so happy then. I was so happy…

"Alan," I reminded myself aloud, attempting to return my thoughts to the present. I had a real live guy with great arms that cared for me right here in Penticton. Skinny as a rail, hardly noticeable, Alan Swift, had blossomed after high school. On the shyer side, he'd discovered weightlifting as a physical activity he could do by himself. His friends quickly noticed the changes in his body and before long several of them were also pumping iron in his basement. When he'd inherited a small warehouse down near the marina, Alan opened Swift's Gym. The burgeoning fitness craze, a fantastic location and Alan's seemingly miraculous change soon had locals flocking to his business. Alan himself, was the best advertising for Swift's Gym; a walking billboard. I remembered the day I first saw the new Alan. I hadn't recognized him until he'd spoken with me. The transformation had been stunning. Inside that muscular frame, however, I'd found the same sweet boy I used to play with in grade school. Our romance was blossoming, too. Alan had been so patient, understanding how difficult it had become for me to trust anyone, let alone another man. Alan stayed at work late and closed the gym Thursday nights or I might be snuggled in those arms right now.

My thoughts securely restored to the here and now, I headed out to join Mom on the deck. I knew there would be extra glasses waiting by a pitcher of Okanagan Bliss. I'd heard the blender whirling, while I was on the phone. Mom blended together a heavenly concoction made up of fresh fruits and rum that she called Okanagan Bliss. It went down very easily and really was blissful. Spring evenings, like this one, it wasn't unusual for one or two of our friends to come by and watch the sun set over the lake with us.

The weather-spoiled locals all complained that 2018/19 had been the longest winter in memory, followed by, curse upon curse, the crappiest spring ever. I hadn't noticed. No one could possibly complain about the last few weeks, however. For me, every day of freedom had been a glorious day.

"Pull up a chair," Mom said as I approached the patio table. Her chaise lounge was semi-reclined and pointing at the lowering sun.

I'd barely aimed mine and sat down before I heard Rhonda's motorbike pull into our driveway. A minute later she appeared at the edge of the deck bearing a bottle of rum and a bag of fruit.

"Next batch is on me," she cheerfully announced. "Good evening, Liz. You too, Butthead."

"Beavis," I lamely replied. Rhonda and I joked and clowned around so much at the office that Mrs. Litmus, the stodgy receptionist, began calling us Beavis and Butthead. After a spirited best four of seven match of Ro-sham-bo, that Rhonda somehow won, she claimed the Beavis portion of the nickname, leaving me stuck with Butthead.

I awoke the next morning, barely hung over, still feeling good about Barb and Brian. That didn't last long. As I made my way down to the basement to see how the renovations had progressed while I was out yesterday, my phone rang. A call this early couldn't be good news. The caller ID showed Buck Henshaw's number, my general contractor.

I'd decided to use my share of the book advance to finish the basement renovation Dad had started many years earlier. I'd modified his simple plan for a rec/game room into a full-fledged one bedroom, one and a half bath, self-contained suite. Drawing up the plans had been a blast. My girlfriends had helped. It turned out that on top of her many other talents, Rhonda had some drafting skills. It was Erika's brilliant idea to add a half bath to the plan and an eating bar in the kitchenette. Hannah helped me pick out colors and materials, while Mom seemed to know of a discount or wholesale place for everything. We'd spent many evenings out on the deck dreaming, drawing and getting pleasantly 'blissed'.

"Good morning, Buck."

"And a very good morning to you, Reggie Girl," he answered. I could hear the perpetual smile through his slight Aussie accent. Tall and lean, with a bushy mustache and eyebrows to match, he reminded me of Tom Selleck in the movie *Quigley Down Under*. Never married and pushing sixty, the confirmed bachelor liked to joke that he'd met plenty of the right women, but he just wasn't the right bloke to get hitched. According to Mom, Buck was never short of female companions. "I wanted to catch you before you took off for your morning bike ride."

"What's up?"

"The electrician got tied up on the Watson job and can't make it until tomorrow."

"The drywall is supposed to go in tomorrow," I said, feeling exasperated. "The flooring guys are supposed to come on Monday."

"Relax, Love," Buck said. "I convinced Bobby to work through the weekend. It cost me a bloody expensive bottle of scotch, though."

"Thanks, Buck," I said, shaking my legs to ease away the melting tension that had instantly risen. Planning the renovation had been far easier than actually doing it. We'd already had a week of delays. Buck was pretty good at rescheduling sub-contractors, but the housing boom had struck the Okanagan in full force and the good sub-trades were in high demand. "Put it on my tab."

"Not necessary, Love," Buck laughed. "I'm likely to drink half of the damn thing anyway. I just wanted you to know, so you didn't worry about things. I promise we'll have you in your new suite by the first."

"Thank you, Buck, you're the best."

"Don't I know it," he laughed again. "I'll pop by on Saturday to check on the progress. Now you go have a good ride. I have a missing plumber to track down."

"I won't be here Saturday," I blurted, just as the line went dead. I didn't know whether he'd heard me or not. I shrugged, realizing that he really didn't need me to be there, he had a key.

The power of suggestion got to me. I'd planned to run with Hannah this morning, but she hadn't shown up. I grabbed my helmet and bike instead. Hannah was never late, so something must have come up at work. Now that she had her detective's shield, Hannah's schedule had become irregular. I knew how that went, having been a police detective myself in a former life. I picked up my cell phone and sure enough, there was a text from Hannah: 'Sorry have to work (poop imogie), talk later'. Crime is often inconvenient.

The bike had been a good choice. I'd have run four to five kilometers at most before turning around and heading back. On my bike I'd gone at least seven K's, on the KVR Trail towards the Village of Naramata, when I spotted several flashing lights off to my left. As I got closer, I counted three police cars, a firetruck and an ambulance.

Curiosity got the best of me. I found a path heading that direction and wound my way toward the lights. I eventually found myself at the impressive timber and wrought iron front gates of the Butterface Winery. I recognized the name from a recent trip to the liquor store. I know that I probably should have been offended, but I'd chuckled when I read the labels; Butterface Wines - Drink two of these, no bag required. They offered a simple choice of red or white wines: Zipper Ripper Red and Bleached Blonde White. At $8.99 per bottle, they were two of the best valued local wines available, according to the woman working in the wine department. I confess to buying the red. It hadn't been half bad. They'd apparently become quite popular with the younger crowd.

The gate was open. I stowed my bike behind the entrance and walked past the monstrously-large two-story home toward all the activity at the out buildings beyond. As I rounded the corner of the house, a massive six car garage came into view. All the doors were closed, but in front of the far bay sat a bright red, very sleek-looking sports car. If I had to guess, I'd have gone

24

with Ferrari. I didn't know much about foreign cars. My dad had been a muscle car guy. When I was a kid, he'd owned a lime green, 1973 Baracuda. Or as Dad and I had called it: 'the 'Cuda' -- still my all-time favorite car.

I'd been right about it being a Ferrari. As I got closer, I could see the dancing horse chrome logo above the bumper. I still didn't know which model, but the thing looked both fast and expensive. I passed by a low, wide building constructed of the same wood and stone as the main house. A sign hanging from the sunshade above the large patio identified it as the wine tasting studio. The front was literally a wall of glass. I glanced behind me and my breath caught in my throat. The building had been situated perfectly, providing a fabulously unobstructed view of Lake Okanagan from Penticton to Peachland. Summerland and Giant's Head Rock loomed directly across the water from here. I'd grown up in the area, but could not remember seeing a more spectacular view of the huge lake than this one. I kicked myself for not having my phone or camera with me. Next time, I vowed.

No one stopped me as I slipped past the idling fire truck to the largest of the out buildings. Made completely of metal, the huge structure was shaped exactly like a traditional country barn. The red walls and green roof helped sell that image. Police milled around the large wide-open roll-up door. I spotted a window off to the side and poked my nose up against the glass just in time to see the ambulance driver wheel a sheet-covered body out. Someone had died.

"Hey," an angry voice shouted from inside. "Get away from there!"

I stepped back, but it was too late. All eyes inside the building instantly turned to look at me through the single pane of glass.

"It's okay, she's with me." Hannah appeared from behind a large metal vat. Besides me, she was the only other person I could see who wasn't wearing some kind of official uniform. She motioned for me to come inside.

"Good morning, Reggie," Officer Hempel said as I stepped through the large opening. I recognized him and a couple of the other cops from the precinct.

"Good morning, Frank," I replied. I removed my bike helmet and went straight to Hannah, nodding a greeting to a couple of the other faces I knew.

"What's a lowly gumshoe doing at my crime scene?" Hannah kidded me, as I approached.

"I figured a flatfoot like yourself could use a hand, since both of yours would be busy searching for your own ass," I responded. I'd been saving that one for the right occasion.

"Yah, yah." She stifled a smile and rolled her eyes. "Sorry about this morning."

"Not to worry," I assured her. "I got your text and figured something important must have come up."

"That's for sure."

"Looks like more than stolen bikes this morning," I said, referencing the last case we'd worked together. Tracking down a local stolen bicycle had led us to a theft ring operating nationally. The well-organized group stole high-end road and mountain bikes, then moved them out of province to cities where they would resell them on Kijiji and Craigslist. They'd been making a fortune until Hannah and I figured it out.

"Milo Getz is dead," Hannah told me.

Where did I know that name from? Suddenly it hit me and the image of the handsome lead singer of Aurora, a popular band from the eighties and nineties, sprang into my head. I'd had their poster on my bedroom wall right between April Wine and the Tragically Hip. I'd felt so cool back then.

"Milo Getz -- the musician?" I asked rhetorically. Hannah nodded. "What was he doing here?"

"This is his place."

"You're kidding."

"All thirty-three acres," she said.

"Of course, Butterface," I said, smacking the side of my head. For some reason, I hadn't made the now obvious connection between the wine label and the name of Aurora's biggest selling album. The CD cover featured a big busted woman in a tight pink cashmere sweater wearing a brown paper bag over her head. I knew this, I'm ashamed to admit, because like most of my friends, I'd owned it. It might still be at the house. Most radio stations refused to play the song, 'She was a Two Bagger', when it first came out, which of course only made it more desirable. Album sales skyrocketed. The things you found offensive later in life were funny and cool when you were a teen. Laurie Henderson wore an identical pink cashmere sweater to school every day for months after the album was released. She filled it out almost as well as the cover model. The boys had certainly noticed her after that. I wondered what had become of her. I made a mental note to ask Mom.

"Yep, one and the same," Hannah confirmed, rolling her eyes.

"I had a big crush on him when I was fifteen."

"Didn't we all?" Hannah chuckled, then quickly got serious. "It appears that Milo was checking the wine in that vat," she pointed to one at the end of a row of huge containers, "slipped, hit his head, and drowned in red wine."

"That was unfortunate."

"One of his employees found him hanging, half-in/half-out, about two hours ago," Hannah explained, then consulted her notes. "Ernesto Rodriguez arrived at work this morning at seven am. He spent an hour and a half cleaning up the tasting room before coming to this building. He came in that man door," she pointed at the same door I'd entered through, "and turned on the lights. That's when he saw the body hanging from the vat. He dragged Getz down, called 9-1-1, and tried to administer CPR - to no avail."

Hannah looked up from her notes. "Rodriguez said that he hadn't realized it was his boss until he was about to start CPR."

"He was alone with the body until the paramedics arrived?" I asked.

"No, Mrs. Getz found out when the ambulance driver buzzed the house for admittance through the front gate and she rushed over ahead of them," Hannah said. "When the paramedics came in she was shaking the body and screaming at her husband to wake up. They had a hard time prying her away from her husband."

"That must have been terrible for her," I said, shaking my head. "How is she doing?"

"She was in shock when I arrived," Hannah told me. "Had to be sedated."

"Poor woman..."

"Yes." Hannah nodded sympathetically. "She was ranting on and on about murder and a conspiracy against her husband."

"That's too bad." Unfortunately, I'd seen this type of reaction from other loved ones of victims before. Senseless death can be a hard concept to grasp. Some fill in the blanks with dark ideas.

"I'm heading up to the house to check on her now," Hannah said.

"Mind if I look around?"

"You know the drill," she reminded me.

"Of course," I assured her. "Don't touch anything and stay out of everyone's way." I watched Hannah give a uniformed cop a task as she left the building. He responded eagerly. It was great seeing Detective Buckley getting the respect she deserved.

I turned my attention to the taped-off area. The cavernous building contained a dozen very large metal vats. The top hatch of the end one hung open wide and several small puddles of red liquid, wine I assumed from the color and location, lay on the polished concrete floor below. A pair of narrow wheels had rolled through the puddles and stained a track leading toward the big door. A tall stepladder stood off to the side with an evidence marker sitting on the top step.

One of the workers had pulled Milo out of the vat and tried to revive him right there. Had he fallen into the vat or had there been foul play as Mrs. Getz believed? An accident seemed much more likely. I could see the techs had already dusted the stepladder and the area around the hatch for prints. I made a wide circle around the vat. There were several rows of neatly-stacked large oak barrels behind each vat. Past the barrels stood six more stainless-steel vats. Obviously newer, these ones had computer monitors attached to them, instead of gauges like the others. Beyond them, the rear of the building contained the bottling equipment and hundreds of crates of empty bottles.

On my seventeenth birthday, I toured a small winery with Mom and Dad and had my first tasting. Dad insisted that I learn about wine, since we lived in the 'Napa Valley of the north' as he used to call the Okanagan. I'd felt like such an adult that day. It's a memory I'll always treasure. After that, during Sunday dinners I 'd have a half a glass of local wine, while Dad, or occasionally Mom, explained the type, vintage and best use for each. At first, the sweet wines like Riesling and Sherry were my favorites, but after a while I began to appreciate the subtle background flavors like oak, plum and cherry in the dryer wines. Each bottle became a mystery to solve and a small adventure to savor. To this day, I don't have a favorite, preferring to try something new.

The Butterface winery was nothing like that first one I'd toured. This was huge and modern by comparison. Lots of metal and chrome. Even the wooden barrels gleamed.

I had to admit the entire place was very neat and clean. A futuristic robotic factory came to mind. The rows of barrels perfectly aligned, the empty bottles stacked with military precision. Then I spotted an anomaly near one of the huge overhead doors. "One of these things is not like the others," Big Bird's song began to play in my head. Off to the side stood half a dozen pallets of bottles that hadn't been put away yet. I hummed along with the Sesame Street character as I wandered over. These crates looked slightly different from the orderly stacked ones against the far wall. As I got closer, I could see that one of them had been opened and a single bottle had been removed. I glanced around but couldn't see the escapee anywhere. Up close, I could immediately tell that these bottles were different from the rest. The shape and size didn't quite match the others. Perhaps that was why they hadn't been put away. There had probably been a shipping error. Mystery solved. Big Bird stopped singing as I returned my thoughts to the dead icon and his music.

As I wandered back toward the front of the building, I caught myself absent-mindedly humming the catchy melody of the 'Two Bagger' song, and thankfully stopped before anybody heard me. The song continued in my head as a crazy thought popped into my head. What if the offensive song had something to do with the singer's death? I dismissed the idea. The song was over twenty years old. I'd been sixteen... Could it really have been that long ago? I stopped in my tracks, the math swirling around in my head. Wow. I'm thirty-seven years old. I don't feel thirty-seven. That means Mom is about to turn sixty. She does not look sixty, not to me, at least. As for myself, brains have always been more important than looks, but I found myself hoping to look that good when I'm her age.

A bulb flash caught my eye, bringing me back to the present. One of the crime scene techs was busy taking pictures of one of two tall oblong wooden tables near the window I'd looked through earlier. The absence of chairs or stools around them suggested they were meant to be stood at. The simple four-legged tables were matt black and on the nearest one sat a plain glass carafe in the center and a single stemless wineglass at one end. Both containers had about a half inch of red wine in them.

I moved closer, but stayed back far enough so as not to get in the woman's way. Her shoulder length midnight hair swayed as she methodically took pictures from every angle. I didn't recognize her, but felt I should. Her dark eyes, high cheekbones and thick lips reminded me of a First Nations girl I'd struck up a friendship with when I was a kid. Audra something?

I felt an overwhelming urge to get a closer look at both her and the table when a hand fell on my shoulder. Instinctively I ducked and spun away; my fists clenched, ready for battle. Some jailhouse habits die hard.

"I'm sorry, Reggie. I should know better," Hannah apologized.

I instantly felt both foolish and bad. Hannah looked mortified even though she'd done nothing wrong. "No, no, it's okay." I produced as big a smile as I could and forced myself to laugh. "It's my fault. No harm, no foul." As if I hadn't already been a little self-conscious, dressed in tight bike shorts and a bright orange t-shirt amongst all these uniforms. I unclenched my fists and patted her on the shoulder. "Did you learn anything from the Mrs.?" I asked, anxious to move on.

"Quite a bit actually," Hannah said. "Mavis Getz is Australian, Tasmanian to be more exact. Met her husband while he was on tour down under. They married less than three weeks later. Travelled all over the world with the band for several years until they bought the winery and settled here."

"Aurora still tours, don't they?"

"According to Mavis, less and less every year," Hannah told me. "In fact, she says Milo didn't want to travel anymore and hadn't performed in a concert for more than a year and a half."

"Really." I knew that some aging rockers toured long after they'd become grandparents. Most of them did not look that great in leather pants anymore, but that didn't seem to stop them.

"They hosted a big barbeque yesterday to celebrate the tenth anniversary of Butterface Wines," Hannah informed me. "Over a hundred guests, a few of which stayed until the wee hours."

"Sounds like Milo could still party like a rock star," I commented.

"Mavis said her husband had always been a night owl. There were only a couple guests left when she finally pulled the plug and went to bed at around 2 am."

"Did she say who was still here?"

"Terry Martin, the vineyard owner next door, and Ross Gregory, the man who sold Milo the winery ten years ago," Hannah continued. "She told me that just before she climbed into bed, she saw Mr. Gregory's car drive off. The lights had been turned off in the tasting center where the party had been, but she could see lights on here in the main barn."

"So it would seem as though Terry Martin was the last man to see Milo alive," I said.

"That's what it looks like," Hannah confirmed. "I'm going next door to speak with him when we're done here."

"How is Mrs. Getz doing?" I wondered.

"She's resting comfortably," Hannah said, returning my smile. "One of the EMT's gave her a sedative and is staying with Mavis until a friend arrives to look after her."

"Inspector Buckley," the tech that had been taking photos of the table, called out. As she turned our way, I could see her whole face clearly for the first time now that her camera wasn't in the way. She really did remind me of Audra. Her dark eyes flashed my direction. I smiled, she didn't.

"Yes, what is it?" Hannah asked.

"Excuse me," she said, stepping between Hannah and me, almost as if resentful of my presence.

"Annabel, this is Reggie Swann," Hannah told her. "She's a PPD consultant."

"I know who she is," the young woman sniped, without looking at me.

Hannah glanced at me, as if to ask what I'd done to offend her CSI tech. I could only shrug, since I hadn't a clue.

"I'm finished with the table," she reported.

"Did you find anything?"

"Nothing definitive," she shrugged. As she turned and lead Hannah to the table I spotted her name tag – Hacquin.

That was why she looked familiar. A girl I'd known during my early school days had been a Hacquin, also. Audra Hacquin was her name. Besides my dad and me, Audra was the only other person I knew with green eyes. While I had mousey blonde hair, hers was coal black, which made her eyes even more striking. We were in the same grade but went to different schools. We'd played soccer against each other throughout middle school and junior high. She'd been such a natural athlete. Graceful and fast – the only girl I played against that could catch up to me when I got a breakaway. Despite being rivals we'd become friends. Though, I had no memories of her beyond the ninth grade. I did recall her telling me that she'd been the oldest of four girls. Annabel must have been one of those younger sisters.

I followed her and Hannah over to the table.

"There are usable prints on this glass but none on the carafe," she told Hannah. We could clearly see where the graphite printing powder had attached itself to the oils left behind by finger tips. Dozens of partial prints, some overlapping, some smeared and a few relatively clear ones covered the glass, while there was very little powder on the carafe, only a couple of thin streaks were visible. "It looks as though it's been wiped down with a dry cloth." I nestled closer and could see that like the glass and carafe, one end of the table's surface had prints while the other side was almost free of graphite.

"It looks like someone, probably the deceased, had a glass of wine at this table," Hannah said, shrugging her shoulders.

"Why are there no prints on the carafe?" I wondered aloud, apparently to myself since neither woman responded.

"Whoever was drinking here," CSI Hacquin told Hannah, "wasn't drinking alone."

"What makes you say that?" Hannah asked.

"Because there are no prints on the carafe," I said louder. "It's been wiped clean."

"You see this," Annabel ignored me and pointed to a palm and partial thumb print on the table near the carafe. In unison, Hannah and I leaned closer.

"It looks like the fingers have been cut off," I blurted out, getting excited that this might be an actual murder scene and not just an unfortunate accident.

Annabel glanced sharply at me, then turned her attention back to Hannah. "That's right. It appears that this entire end of the table has been wiped down along with the carafe. And then there is this," she said, bringing our attention to a small crescent-shaped mark on the empty end of the table. "Even though someone wiped off this end of the table, a small amount of condensation returned where another object, about the same diameter as that one," she nodded toward the glass at the other end of the oblong surface, "had sat for a while."

"I wonder what became of the other glass?" Hannah asked aloud, ducking to glance under the table.

Annabel moved around to the other end of the table. "This is what I speculate may have caused these marks." She pantomimed picking up the carafe, then leaned forward with her empty hand hovering above the partial handprint and pretended to pour some wine into the invisible glass at the other end of the table.

"Makes sense," Hannah agreed.

"It seems strange that someone only wiped that end of the table," I said.

"It is suspicious, although, someone may have started cleaning up and got interrupted," Annabel suggested.

"Is there any way to tell how long that mark or hand print has been there?" Hannah asked.

"Not definitively," Annabel answered, after a few seconds of thought.

"If you had to guess," Hannah prompted.

"You know better than to ask me that, Detective Buckley," Annabel said, with more than a hint of scolding in her tone. "I'm a woman of science, not a psychic."

"Sorry," Hannah apologized. "Anything else?"

"That's it for now," Annabel said. "I'm heading back to the lab. If I find anything else I'll let you know."

I had the urge to ask whether she had a sister named Audra, but Annabel gave me a last derisive glance as if daring me to open my mouth. Taken aback, by her unwarranted hostility I couldn't speak. I could only watch as she strode away.

"What did you do to her?" Hannah asked.

"Nothing that I can think of," I answered honestly. "As far as I know, we've never met before."

"You must have done something," Hannah stated. "She clearly, does not like you."

"I knew a girl, who might have been her sister, when I was a kid..."

"What's going on here?" A man yelled, storming into the building, dressed in tight Levis, a faded but pressed yellow cotton long-sleeved shirt and an undersized straw cowboy hat. On most men, the hat would have looked ridiculous but on him it worked. The perfect contrast to his deeply tanned skin and dark features. "How long has that vat been open like that?" He rushed toward it, almost reaching the ladder before Officer Hempel managed to step in front of him. "I need to get it closed before the whole batch is ruined."

"Sir, this is an active crime scene," Frank informed him.

"I don't care," he responded, deftly sidestepping Frank.

"It's okay, Frank," Hannah called out, as the officer turned to grab him.

The man slid the ladder into place, scurried up the rungs, flipped closed the hatch then hopped back down and checked the gauges on the front of the vat. Shoulders sagged and he took the hat from his head and slammed it against his leg. A loud, "Damn it," sprang from his lips. Then he noticed the crime scene tape next to him. As he turned around, his eyes danced from one person to another, noticing for the first time since his arrival that most of the strangers surrounding him were cops, before settling on Officer Hempel. "Wait, what are you talking about? A crime scene?"

Hannah stepped forward. "We're not certain a crime has been committed, but I'm afraid there's been a horrible accident."

"Milo Getz is dead," Hempel stated.

"No," the man moaned, visibly shaken by the news. "There must be some mistake." His eyes filled with tears. He choked up, unable to speak for the better part of a minute. When he recovered his voice a flood of information sprang forth.

Roman Angelo turned out to be Butterface Winery's master vintner. Getz had hired him the day after buying the vineyard. Today was his tenth anniversary with the company. According to Mr. Angelo, Milo had treated him like a partner from that first day and the distraught man considered Milo to be his closest friend. The master vintner told Hannah that together he and the Getz's had made the label one to be proud of. Apparently, both Milo and his wife, Mavis, were very involved in the business. Milo not only did a great job promoting the wine inside and outside the winery but had named the wines and designed the labels himself. The vines were Mrs. Getz's domain. She oversaw the planting, care and harvest of them. The making of the wine itself was left to Roman. He prided himself on producing a consistent product that tasted the same bottle after bottle, year after year. Sales of Butterface Wines had grown by leaps and bounds in recent years. They were now the second largest seller of Okanagan wines and the label was rapidly becoming one of the most recognized nationally. Big plans to both expand the product line and the vineyard itself were well underway.

As Hannah and I continued to question him, the techs and other cops wrapped things up and began vacating the premises.

As informative as he'd been about the operations, unfortunately, Roman had little new information that could help about the events that led up to Milo's accident. He had been to the party and BBQ the previous day, but had left quite early to join his brother and sister-in-law who were coincidentally celebrating their wedding anniversary on the same day. I had to stifle a chuckle when Mr. Angelo informed us that his brother, Michael, was a painter. A house painter, but a painter none the less.

When we'd finished the interview, Roman immediately rushed to the house to console the widow Getz.

Hannah gave me a ride to the front gate, where I'd left my bike. We made plans to run together the next morning, then she headed off to interview Terry Martin, the neighbor.

CHAPTER 4

Even though I arrived through the back gate, I could see the corner of a Home Depot delivery truck sitting in the driveway. I chained my bike to the rear step rail, rushed in through the back door and raced through the house, hoping that my kitchen cabinets had arrived. Where I normally parked Betsy, the garage was loaded with large boxes, the kind that would hold cabinetry – hopefully, cream-colored shakers from the Martha Stewart collection. I was anxious to get a look inside the large boxes. I'd need a utility knife and I knew where to find one.

I'd just reached Dad's old tool case when I heard voices out front. I grabbed a knife and then wriggled my way towards them, just in time to see a stocky delivery guy haul himself into the driver's seat, while Mom hugged the other one.

"Thanks for the iced tea, Mrs. Swann," he said, releasing her.

"You say hello to your mom for me, Phillip," my mom told him. "Tell her I'll stop in for a visit next time I'm in Kelowna."

"Thanks guys," I called, as I emerged from the garage. "Do I need to sign anything?"

"No, your mom took care of it," Phillip said, his casual demeanor becoming business-like as I approached. This was the second time today I was getting the cold-shoulder treatment. "All the packages arrived and were delivered damage free, Ma'am."

"I checked them as they were unloaded," Mom confirmed.

"Excellent," I said. "Thank you, so much."

"The install crew is booked and will be here at 8 am Monday morning," Phillip assured me, and climbed up into the truck cab. "Have a nice day, ladies." We both waved as the truck backed out of the driveway. Phillip smiled directly at Mom and waved back.

"What was that about?" I asked Mom, after they drove off.

"What do you mean?"

"He clearly didn't like me."

"Apparently, someone has been calling every day for the past two weeks demanding to know where these cabinets were and when they would be delivered." Mom looked at me accusingly.

"Well, it wasn't me."

"Really?"

"Really," I assured her. "It must have been Mary, Buck's assistant. She runs his office while Buck is out checking on worksites and chasing down sub-contractors. Besides, looking after Accounts Payable and Receivable she must order the building supplies. She must have been the one calling."

"That makes sense," Mom said. "The squeaky wheel always gets the grease."

"And those guys thought I was the squeaky wheel." I shook my head.

"I guess so." Mom threw her arm around my shoulder. "It doesn't really matter, and look at the bright side..."

"What's that?" I asked, still felling a little miffed at being labeled the bad guy.

"Well, darling, your cabinets are here on time."

"Damn right," I agreed, instantly feeling better. I pulled the knife out of my pocket. "Let's take a look at them."

I carefully cut a one foot square hole in the front of the closest box. I breathed a sigh of relief when I confirmed that they were in fact the correct color and style.

"They are going to look beautiful, Sweetheart," Mom said, brushing her fingers across the door.

"I hope so." The only renovation I'd previously been a part of had been refurbishing the family boat when I was thirteen. I didn't remember that experience being this stressful.

After a shower and some lunch I called Buck's cell to let him know that the cabinets had arrived. Again, he assured me that the electrician would get the wiring finished over the weekend.

I jumped on Betsy and headed to work. By the time I reached the office, my building woes were far behind me. I got right to work on a skip trace that had been giving me some trouble. A twenty-five-year-old woman masquerading as Jennifer Gleason had rented an apartment in Okanagan Falls in June of last year. The identity thief amassed a small mountain of debt, including a loan on a new Nissan Altima, before driving it off into the sunset two week before the real Manitoba native and her father came to town to face the angry creditors who had begun calling.

It turned out that fake Jennifer had been real Jennifer's student at the college where she taught evening classes in Thompson, Manitoba. The two had struck up a friendship that extended beyond the classroom. There, she'd been calling herself Holly Brown. Real Jennifer had been sorry to see Holly move back to Thunder Bay, where she was needed to care for her ailing mother. A few days ago, two RCMP officers and the real Holly Brown had come around looking for an imposter who had stolen her identity and ruined her credit. Real Holly Brown had turned out to be a middle-aged, divorced, dental hygienist, who had lived next to a student who'd perfectly matched the description of our serial identity thief.

Faux Jennifer or FJ, as I'd begun to call her, had left a haphazard trail of debt, spoiled credit ratings and broken hearts in her wake, including several boyfriends and at least two fiancés. As I discovered more identities, patterns began to emerge. Usually, after stealing both the identity and often the resume of her female victims, FJ moved from one medium-sized center to another, avoiding large cities where creditors were prone to quicker action, and smaller towns where it was difficult to maintain a low profile. Here, she'd taught a Creative Fiction class at Okanagan College in Penticton. In Thompson, as Holly Brown, she'd taken a job as a dental hygienist. By all accounts, she'd been well-liked and competent. Assuming the identity of Maria Garber, FJ had managed a shoe store in Thunder Bay, where, after she skipped town they'd soon discovered a considerable amount of missing inventory. Plus, in each case that the RCMP had investigated, she'd borrowed money from whatever poor sap she'd been dating, just before disappearing.

Real Jennifer's father hired me to track down fake Jennifer, who by now, almost certainly had become someone else. Fortunately, for us FJ had made a small mistake.

Locally, I'd found three likely candidates for FJ's next identity. She'd become good friends with each of them. My money was on Christine Lake, a high school Literature teacher who lived right across the street. From the information I'd gathered, FJ had been an enthusiastic and very well liked instructor at the college. Christine described FJ as well read and helpful. She'd even pitched in and corrected assignments on occasion.

The new school year had already begun across most of the provinces and no new teachers named Christine Lake had surfaced yet. Neither of the other two identities had thrown up any red flags, either.

Though the regular data bases hadn't turned up any information on FJ's whereabouts so far, I wasn't about to give up. The prolific dater had also bilked several young and middle-aged men out of cash and gifts throughout the Okanagan before her hasty departure. I suspected she would continue this behavior. For the past couple of days I'd been scouring dating websites looking for a similar profile to one she had used locally.

I'd studied the profiles of her many boyfriends and discovered that FJ had a "type": not overly handsome, usually shy and always in a career that paid well. During interviews with her suitors the words 'she was the best thing that ever happened to me' invariably came up. Working long hours and caring about her students, perhaps a little too much, made her less accessible than her suitors would have liked, otherwise FJ had been the perfect girlfriend. Reality proved FJ to be less concerned about work and students -- instead juggling two or three happy and generous boyfriends at all times. In each case, faux Jennifer pretended to be struggling with finances due to an ailing mother, mounting credit card debt or something along those lines. Each beau had happily given or lent her five to ten thousand dollars.

This woman had to be stopped.

Who knew there were so many online dating sites? Using an amalgamation of FJs former lovers, I'd put together a profile of a lovable loser with a good job and had dropped the bait into dozens of potential destinations where I felt FJ might next set up shop. Now I was busy trolling through the many responses, nudges and winks hoping she'd bite.

I'd just discounted a promising response from a lonely woman in Prince George when my intercom buzzed.

"Miss Swann you have a visitor at the front desk," the law firm's starchy receptionist announced. To be fair, after our rocky start, Mrs. Litmus tried to tolerate my presence even though I wasn't exactly with the firm. Efficient and conscientious, she was a great guardian of the office. At a glance she could tell if someone had real business to discuss. Though, a year earlier, I'd been the exception.

"Thank you, Frances. I'll be right out," I responded, knowing that she preferred using formal names. I was the newbie in our little pack and she'd been subtly trying to remind me that I was the low dog on the totem pole. Sometimes I almost felt sorry for Mrs. Litmus. Almost. There had been too many changes at the firm for her liking. She'd been manning that desk for twenty-five years, managing the schedules and appointments of the now retired Mr. Green and Mr. Garrison. Erika was far less dependent than her father and his partner had been, arranging her own schedule. And to top things off, there was now a private investigator holding shop in Mr. Green's old office. The horror... Plus, I think it annoyed Mrs. Litmus that Erika, Rhonda and I had bonded so quickly.

I hadn't been expecting a visitor. I pulled my notes together and slid them into the heavy mahogany desk's top drawer, before heading out to greet my guest. Sitting in reception was a woman with such an angelic face, that puffy rings around her eyes could not hide her beauty.

"I'm Reggie Swann," I announced, as I came around the front desk.

"Thank you for seeing me," the woman said, with a decidedly Australian accent. "I'm Mavis Getz."

At the mention of her name, Mrs. Litmus and I glanced at each other.

"Are you perhaps looking for a lawyer, Mrs. Getz?" the gatekeeper queried.

"No, as I said, I'm here to see Miss Swann."

"I'm so sorry for your loss, Mrs. Getz. Please come with me to my office," I said, guiding her past the front desk. I shot a triumphant smirk at Mrs. Litmus.

"What can I do for you, Mrs. Getz?" I asked after we'd gotten settled into opposite ends of the comfy leather couch I'd inherited with the rest of the office furniture.

"Please call me Mavis," she said. "May I call you Reggie?"

"Of course, Mavis."

"Thank you, Reggie. Let me get right to the point then," she told me, leaning forward and locking her large amber eyes onto mine. Her hair was the same color. If her lashes and eye-brows hadn't perfectly matched, I'd have assumed she'd colored it. "My husband was murdered. I need you to find his killer."

CHAPTER 5

I'd read the coroner's report. Wine had been found in the victim's lungs and there was a large contusion on the top of his head. Together, the coroner and Hannah concluded that the most likely scenario had been that the heavy metal hatch on the vat had fallen forward, hitting Milo on the head, rendering him unconscious. The musician fell forward, his head submerged in liquid and he had drowned. The death had been ruled accidental. I knew that Hannah would be releasing the official findings later today.

The half-wiped table and fingerprint-less carafe had turned out to be the only suspicious evidence at the scene and there were plausible explanations for them. Milo had a pair of leather gloves tucked into his back pocket. He might have been wearing the gloves when he carried the glass container to the table. It was also not only possible but quite likely that he had wiped the end of the table himself and then become distracted by something before finishing.

An unfortunate and tragic mishap, to be sure, but murder? A surge of pity added to the sympathy I already felt for the distraught woman in front of me. After two days, Mavis Getz was still trying to add reason to her husband's senseless death. At least she appeared to be calm and rational.

"I know that the police are ready to declare his death accidental," Mavis said, sitting back in the chair. Her red-rimmed eyes hadn't wavered from mine. "Despite my many protests, I might add."

"What makes you think that Milo was murdered?" I asked, mostly to be polite. Plus, despite the circumstances, I loved listening to her charming accent.

"I don't think he was murdered, Love, I know it."

"I'm listening," I assured her.

Her eyes finally released from mine. She stood and began pacing. "Some of this might sound crazy, but I assure you it is not."

"After all that I've been through, Mavis, I promise to give you the benefit of the doubt," I told her.

"First of all, Milo knows... excuse me," she paused as a tear escaped her eye. I pushed a box of tissues her way. "Thank you," she said, composing herself. "I'm still getting used to the idea that he's gone. Milo knew almost nothing about making wine. He left all the production to Roman."

"With all that wine around he wouldn't be tempted to dip a glass in once in a while?"

"Didn't drink wine. He pretended to, for marketing purposes, but Milo was a beer guy through and through," Mavis explained, then a smile crossed her face. "He especially liked Cascade Premium. He used to say that Cascade Beer was the second best thing ever exported from Tasmania."

"What was the best thing?" I couldn't help asking.

"Me, he always told everyone." She wiped away another tear and sat back down. "He was such a sweetheart, my Milo. Always singing little love sonnets to me that he'd make up on the spot and forever giving me goofy little gifts." She tugged on the fine gold chain around her neck until a tiny plastic figurine appeared from inside her blouse. She leaned forward so I could see the cute, cartoon Tasmanian Devil surrounded by a heart. At the same time I noticed that the nearly invisible chain and a simple gold band around her ring finger were the only pieces of jewelry Mavis had on. I glanced at her earlobes, and noticed a lack of piercing holes.

"He was such a gentleman, too," she continued. "A woman never opened a door herself if Milo was near."

It was hard for me to reconcile the hard-partying, womanizing rock-star image the media had always portrayed with the man she was describing.

"I'm sorry, I've gotten off topic," Mavis said, as she tucked away her necklace.

"No, that's quite alright," I assured her.

"As I was saying, Milo knew nothing about wine production, so he wouldn't have opened a hatch to check inside for any reason I can think of. Besides, he would never have climbed that ladder."

"Why?" I felt the unmistakable tingle of an unsolved mystery begin work its way up my spine. She had my full attention.

"Two and a half years ago, when the band toured Europe," Mavis explained, "Milo fell off a stage in Belgium."

"I recall reading something about that," I added. "They had to cancel some shows and cut the tour short."

"The truth is, Milo hasn't been on a raised stage since that night," Mavis told me, as if sharing a secret. "The fall broke an eardrum and damaged his inner ear. His balance was compromised. He became deathly afraid of heights."

"That was only a six foot ladder," I said referring to the one by the vats.

"It could have been a step stool and Milo wouldn't have used it," she insisted. "He wouldn't do stairs of any kind. Before the accident, we had a small raised platform in the tasting room for Milo to perform on. About this high," she said, holding her hand about ten inches above the desk top. "After the accident he would not step on it. We took it out. We had to have the house renovated, moving the master bedroom to the main level."

"I had no idea." I'd never read or heard anything about him having a fear of heights. Almost sub-consciously, I lifted a notepad and pen from the nearby coffee table and wrote Milo Getz on the top page. Much to my own surprise, I'd already joined the 'Milo Getz Murder Conspiracy Club'. As far as I knew, the entire membership was seated in my office. I jotted down his overwhelming fear of heights at the top of the first page. "No wonder he hadn't toured in so long."

"With his blessing Aurora quietly tried to find a new lead singer," Mavis told me, "but it was next to impossible to replace Milo. They gave up the idea after a few months."

I couldn't imagine Aurora without Milo. I doubted many people could.

"Plans were underway for a North American tour of smaller, more intimate venues," she said, regret evident in her face. "Places without raised stages. Aurora Unplugged, they were going to call it. Milo was excited. The lads and their wives were going to come here for a month of rehearsals before starting the twenty-five city tour. It would have been like old times." Mavis twisted the tissue in her wringing hands, her voice becoming a whisper. "Instead, they'll be coming here for his funeral."

I reached across the desk and patted her nearest hand. "It will get easier, I promise."

"Sorry Love," Mavis forced a smile.

"The funeral is going to be here?" I asked. The media had been posing this question and speculating since Milo's death. Most expected it to be held in Sudbury, his hometown.

"Milo may have bought the vineyard for me. You see, growing grapes is in my blood. My family owns a vineyard in Tasmania. Yet out of all the places he'd been, all over the world, Milo swore this little slice of heaven was his favorite. I plan to spread his ashes across all four corners of the vineyard."

"What about you?" I asked. "Will you go back to Tasmania?"

"This is my home now," Mavis said. "Roman and I will try to carry on Milo's vision for Butterface Wines."

"I thought that Milo didn't know anything about wine." I'd already scribbled that into my notes.

"He didn't," Mavis said. "He left the vines to my care and the winemaking to Roman, but the marketing was all his. He came up with the names, designed the labels and ran the ad campaigns himself. Milo's artistic side wasn't limited to music. He tirelessly promoted both our and the region's wine whenever and wherever he could."

"Do you know of anyone who would want Milo dead?"

"Obviously, the lyrics of some of his songs didn't sit well with everyone," Mavis conceded. "He'd gotten hundreds, perhaps thousands of angry letters from women's groups over the years, but they've died down in recent years. He tried to keep it from me, but I know he'd received the occasional death threat."

"Did he keep any of them?" I asked, as I made notes under the heading of enemies.

"I doubt it, but I can check if you'd like," Mavis told me. "He didn't take them seriously. Milo had written 'Two Bagger' out of spite, after his first love broke up with him. He regretted recording it, but that song and the Butterface album became such huge hits he and the band almost had no choice but to embrace the bad boy persona and run with it."

"Do you know her name?" I asked. "The girl he wrote the song about."

"Oh, yes," Mavis smiled. "Milo and I had no secrets. Jenna Britain broke his heart. Jenna was literally the girl next door when Milo was growing up. Best friends and each other's first love, first kiss, first everything."

I wrote her name on the pad. "Was there still some animosity between the two of them?"

"Heavens no." Mavis shook her head. "She is a lovely woman. We've become dear friends over the years."

"Still, having a song like 'Two Bagger' written about you, must be difficult to live with," I pondered.

"Believe me, no one would ever put a bag over that woman's head," Mavis chuckled. "The song was ironic. Milo used to laugh and say, 'how lucky he was to have found the two most beautiful girls in the whole world. One lived right next door to him and the other was in the far corner of the world'. At any rate he wasn't wrong about Jenna, she's a true-blue beauty, that one."

I got the distinct impression from her tone and facial expressions that this woman truly did not think of herself as beautiful, though quite clearly, she was. I had to admire that about her.

"When is the last time you saw Jenna?"

"She and her husband, Tom, were at the anniversary party," she told me. "The Britains live in Oshawa, but Tom's parents retired here to Kelowna. They timed a visit, so they could attend."

"Did anything unusual happen, any arguments, disagreements?"

"No..." Mavis' smooth forehead wrinkled for a few seconds. She wasn't wearing any makeup that I could see, and the wrinkles ruled out Botox. I tried to guess her age. She could have passed for twenty-six or twenty-seven, but I knew she'd been married to Milo for fifteen years. So I calculated that she had to be in her mid to late thirties, at least. This woman was roughly my age. Where were the crow's feet and brow lines? Great plastic surgery? Everything about her looked authentic to me. Great genes, I decided as she began to speak again, "... there was nothing. We all had a lovely visit."

"Do you know what time they left the party?" I enquired.

"Right around ten-thirty," Mavis told me, a smile lighting up her face. "It was about the same time as Darryl Lansing, our Maritime distributor, had to leave. Very funny bloke, that Darryl. He told the four of us a story about one of his customers that had us all in stitches, especially Milo."

The smile faded. Her eyes closed, spilling the sudden tears that had formed. I grabbed the box of tissues, set them onto her lap, and then put my hand on her quaking shoulder. I could feel her anguish. I was no stranger to loss and felt my own eyes begin to burn.

"I'm sorry," she said, composing herself. "Several guests left around that time, including the three of them."

I added Darryl's name next to Jenna and Tom. Friends to Mavis, were suspects to me. I questioned her for several more minutes adding two dozen more names of people she'd seen Milo chatting with at the party. I'd be running background checks on everyone at the party, but these names would get special attention. The job wasn't quite as easy, now that I was no longer a cop. But if you knew where to look, and I did, the internet could provide a wealth of information.

"Did Milo have any enemies?"

"Not that I can think of," Mavis said.

"What about in the music industry?"

Mavis raised her eyebrows as she thought for a few seconds, then shrugged and shook her head.

"No rivalry's, feuds or disputes with anyone?"

She responded with another head shake.

"How about locally?"

"Not really," Mavis said, but I could see there was something. "Well, there were a few knockers, but that was donkey years back."

"Knockers?"

"Sorry, complainers and critics," she explained. "It's hardly worth mentioning, but when we first started the Butterface label a few, well, most of the winemakers in the area, formed a coalition to have our wine banned from the shelves. They thought we were trying to make a joke out of the industry, but that was never our intention."

"They obviously weren't successful or you wouldn't still be here," I said, adding knockers to my notes.

"Quite the opposite," Mavis chuckled, though it was mixed with sadness. "Milo always contended that negative publicity was the best kind. He milked it for all it was worth. We couldn't keep up with demand."

"It was the album all over again," I commented.

"Exactly right," Mavis agreed. "After a couple of seasons, the group disbanded. I think they realized that we weren't just a couple of bludgers, here on a lark."

I didn't exactly know what a bludger was, but I got the general drift of her meaning. The coalition she spoke of had caught my attention. "Can you tell me who was in this group against Butterface?"

"It was almost all the winemakers on the eastern benches, plus a few others," Mavis said, shaking her head. "Water under the bridge, though. Like I said, they disbanded years ago when they realized we were serious producers. Most of them were at the bash the other night. Terry Martin, next door to us, organized the whole thing. He was the most vocal at the time, now he's one of Milo's closest friends. Was one of his..."

Tears filled her eyes once again. By the time she grabbed another tissue, they were pouring down her cheeks. She attempted a smile, but full-fledged sobs took over the woman. I pulled her close and let her cry on my shoulder. When the sobs subsided, we stood. I quickly swept aside a tear of my own. Inside, I empathized with the grieving widow. I knew how gut wrenching it could be to lose someone precious to you.

"Will you help me, Reggie?" she asked, her huge sad eyes pleading like a lost child's.

"I promise to look into it," I assured her. Her face brightened and this time she threw her arms around me.

"Thank you, you're true blue," she whispered, into my ear.

I walked her out, where I was relieved to find a taxi waiting. She wasn't in the best condition to drive herself. Mavis politely declined my offer to come by and check on her later, explaining that she had friends staying at the house to keep her company. As I watched the cab drive away, my heart ached for the poor woman.

There was something else, too. As I turned to go back into the office, I felt a sudden chill and was covered with goosebumps, despite the warmth of this lovely day. The very same sensations that used to hit me when I'd been assigned to a new homicide. There was nothing quite like the challenge of solving a murder. Though I couldn't yet say with certainty, that Milo Getz had been murdered, my suspicions had been aroused.

If the rock star really had been murdered, I silently vowed to solve it for his grieving widow.

CHAPTER 6

I returned to my office intending to continue the search for Faux J, but my thoughts kept returning to Mavis Getz. She'd lost her soulmate. I'd gone through that. It does get easier with time, but there would be a hole in her soul that will never close completely. Trent, my ex-husband, remarried six years ago and I still wasn't completely over him. I doubted I ever would be. Trent, had abandoned me and even though, rationally I understood his need to move on with his life, emotionally I never would. The deepest cut of all had been from my own father.

I'd idolized my dad. Growing up, I'd followed him around like a puppy. I'd spent ten times as much time in the garage with him than I had in the kitchen with Mom. Before Dad died, he'd stopped coming to visit me in prison. He could no longer take seeing me in there, my mother had tried to explain. I admit, the first few years inside, I'd been a mess. I'd often been covered in cuts and bruises or had been in the infirmary when they arrived.

When my father passed, I hadn't seen him for over two years. During that time, I'd both missed him and resented his absence. By the end, he drank and smoked heavily and shunned his friends. He'd become a shut-in who'd barely interact with Mom. She came home one day, found him sitting in his easy chair with a cigarette smoldering in his lifeless lips. His heart had quit.

Life had been just as difficult for Mom, maybe worse given Dad. Yet, my mother had never missed a visit and had kept advocating for my freedom despite every set back and road block placed before her. For many years, it seemed as though she was the only person in the country who believed I was innocent. Her faith in me was unshakeable. I owe her my freedom and my life. Her belief in me and her visits had given me the strength, and perhaps more importantly, a reason to make it back to my cell every night.

Then, when the first person I'd dated after getting out of prison turned out to be a serial killer, I'd had to question my judgement of the male gender. Alan Swift helped in this regard. I'd been going out with him for the last three months. Funny, easy on the eyes and most definitely all man, he'd been just what the doctor ordered. It was a good thing Alan was patient and persistent. I'd turned him down half a dozen times before agreeing to go out with him. Earning my trust was no easy thing and he'd been a very good sport about taking things slowly.

Mavis Getz loved her husband, that had been obvious from the way she spoke about him. Since Mavis's visit, I'd begun to see Milo as a real person rather than a guitar-smashing rock icon. Okay, I'd never seen or heard of him actually breaking a guitar, but I'm pretty sure they all did it. I'd never gotten the chance to meet him personally and after hearing his widow describe Milo I felt cheated in that respect.

Death causes a person to examine life. If Mom hadn't brought it up a few weeks earlier, the anniversary of my release would have slipped by without my notice. Time seemed to fly by rapidly on this side of the penitentiary walls. It occurred to me that I no longer kept a running count of the days, as I had for so long. From the time of my arrest, I'd spent eleven months and twelve days in jail awaiting my trial, then another eight years nine months and seven days in prison. All totaled, three thousand, five hundred and forty-six days behind bars. On the inside, the days were long and dreary regardless of the weather. February had been my favorite month, though, slightly less so during leap years. I tried not to keep track. Hadn't wanted to. But like everyone else inside, I couldn't help it. Slightly less than ten years. Almost a decade. Life stood still when you were locked up, while everyone and everything on the outside raced forward, seemingly at the speed of light.

When I first got out, I resented all the changes that had happened while I was inside. Oddly, one of the first differences I noticed was that every second vehicle on the road seemed to be a Sport Utility Vehicle. And since when had Korean vehicles become so popular? There seemed to be more foreign cars on the road than domestic now. At least Ford had started building Mustangs worthy of the marque once again.

Cell phones had gotten huge again, amazingly thin I admit, but some are gigantic. Before my incarceration I'd just gotten the latest greatest tiniest flip phone. Of course, these new monstrosities are basically little computers and high-definition video cameras that you can also make a phone call with, for those of us not savvy enough to skype. So far, the extent of my texting shorthand was limited to 'LOL'. Everything had gotten smarter it seemed. Cars could parallel park themselves. Television had changed. Channel surfing was gone. I used to like flipping through the stations until something caught my eye. To me, scrolling through a menu of hundreds of stations doesn't offer the same excitement. Then when I do find something to watch, Mom's television suggests other programs that I might like. Okay, not all the recent technologies were annoying. I must confess, now that I've figured out how to use my new coffee maker, having a cup of medium roast waiting for me when I get up in the morning has been pretty nice.

Social media had happened. At first, I avoided all forms of it like the plague, then Hannah helped me set up a website for Black Swann Investigations, followed by a personal Facebook page. Thanks mostly to the news coverage of my release and exoneration, plus my assistance in catching the TransCanada Killer, I have ninety thousand online 'friends'. She'd been trying to convince me that I needed a presence on Twitter to help build my brand. I'd never thought of myself as a brand, but maybe I'll give it a shot.

My thoughts turned back to Milo Getz. I wondered if he had loved his wife as much as she seemed to love him. I pulled the Milo Getz notebook from the desk drawer and flipped it open. I wrote mistress with a question mark under the suspect list, which already included most of the winemakers in the Okanagan and all the feminists in Canada. I reluctantly added Mrs. Getz' name to the already large suspect pool. If Milo had indeed been murdered and the crime scene staged to look like an accident, I doubted that Mavis or many other women, for that matter, could have tugged a one hundred and eightyish pound man up a ladder and stuffed him into the vat alone. I tried to imagine myself accomplishing the feat. Even with all my physical training, I doubted I could do it. Some men couldn't either, I realized. Alan could, of course, but he wasn't ordinary. Had there been an accomplice? Roman Angelo popped into my head. The man was young and fit. I penciled his name right below Mavis Getz.

If you can figure out the motive, the crime will often solve itself. Who had the most to gain with Milo gone? On the top of the next page I added the two biggest motivators of all: love and money. I didn't know which it was or if for certain a murder had been committed. One way or the other I'd get answers.

Money was definitely the major influence in my other case. I closed the notebook and finally got back to my online search for FJ.

Hours slipped by. Looking at all these lives boiled down to a picture and a few lines of self-description was both interesting and tedious at the same time. I'd promised myself only five more minutes of it thirty minutes ago. I was about to close out of the Christian/Rural dating site I'd been surfing and call it a day when a profile from Canmore, Alberta caught my eye. Simpler makeup, darker hair and glasses had changed FJ's appearance considerably, but that perfected happy, yet vulnerable-looking smile looked very familiar. I couldn't be 100% certain this was my girl, but my gut told me I'd found her.

She wasn't calling herself Christine Lake as I'd expected. Mary Beth Walker had recently moved to Alberta. A small town girl, who among other things, enjoyed line dancing and baking bread. She'd listed 'My Friend Flicka' as her favorite book of all time. Mary Beth hoped to meet a Christian man who also enjoyed horseback riding and fishing. I would need the right bait to reel in this fisher of men and money.

I'd have to add a little country to the fake profile I'd already posted on a few other sites. I knew the perfect place to take some countrified pictures of my handsome 'buckaroo'. I called Alan as I left the office to see if he had a plaid shirt, a beat up baseball cap and time to do a little modelling in the morning. After some coaxing, that may have included some not so veiled hints at carnal rewards for his participation, Alan agreed to pose as Cattleman Mike for me. He really was a good boyfriend. My heart skipped a beat or two as I imagined his firm bubble-shaped butt wrapped in Wranglers. Paying off Alan for his help would be no hardship.

I'd also need to find and get into contact with the real Mary Beth Walker before FJ ruined her life. Convincing her and her creditors to go along with my sting operation would be crucial to catching the serial con-woman.

CHAPTER 7

I parked Betsy in the garage and went around back to the basement entry. I didn't expect to see any changes from when I'd left, but to my surprise bundles of wire, a stack of electrical boxes and a pair of tool belts were visible through a newly-installed French door. The door looked as good as I'd hoped it would and Buck had obviously found the replacement electricians he'd promised.

"I love you Buck," I said aloud. The handset hadn't yet been mounted on the new door which meant I couldn't go in and look around without prying off the temporary brace that served as a lock. The stairway from the main floor down was being rebuilt. I could wait. There'd been progress and that fact made me happy.

I found Mom in the kitchen, at the stove, happily bopping to the steady beat of an Aurora tune on the radio. Both Mom and Dad had disliked this music when it first came out twenty years before. Ever since the lead singer's death, Milo's story and his music had dominated the television and radio airwaves.

The earthy scents of roasting onions and garlic wafted towards me. "Something smells good in here."

"Hi Darling," Mom said without turning. "Did you see your new door?"

"Yes, it looks great," I answered, lightly kissing the side of her neck as I peeked over her shoulder to see what culinary masterpiece Mom was cooking up. Below I could see a colorful mixture of vegetables. There were pieces of red and yellow peppers, broccoli, squash, onions and mushrooms tumbling around the large pan. She had a gift, my mom. She never used recipes. Cooked by the seat of her pants using whatever ingredients happened to be close at hand and everything she made always tasted wonderful. Unfortunately, I hadn't inherited that gene. I was a recipe girl. I followed them to the tee and yet they never seemed to turn out the same way twice. That had always made me nervous when I cooked for others.

"This smells heavenly," I remarked. "What spices did you use?"

"Actually, none," Mom said, still swaying to the music. "I was going to add some fresh rosemary but these onions I got from Mrs. Paul at the farmers market yesterday are just so sweet I decided not to bother. Unless you think I should?"

"No, no," I protested. "I'm sure it's perfect the way it is." I washed my hands and began setting the table. Sautéed vegetables and brown rice wasn't normal dinner fair while Dad was alive. He'd been a meat and potatoes guy. Most meals were beef or pork with mashed, roasted, or on special occasions, scalloped potatoes, plus peas, corn or carrots and sometimes two or all three mixed together. Like most good Catholics, Fridays had been fish day. A meatless meal would have been considered sacrilegious around our house while I was growing up.

Dad also had a sweet tooth, especially for fruit pies. Mom didn't disappoint there, either. We lived in the right part of the world for that, having fresh-from-the-tree cherries, peaches, and a dozen different varieties of apples. For a change of pace we'd occasionally have strawberry, raspberry, rhubarb or

Mom's personal preference -- a strawberry/rhubarb combo. Cherry got my nod, while Dad had always claimed that the one on the end of his fork, no matter which flavor, was the best he'd ever had.

Dinner tasted even better than it smelled. I swore to myself that I'd duplicate the simple recipe when I cooked a meal for Alan, a vegetarian. If it turned out even half as good as Mom's, we'd both be impressed. He'd had me over for several dinners and I promised to return the favor when my place got finished.

I'd decided to begin my investigation into Milo's death by talking with one of the last people to see him alive: his neighbor, Terry Martin. I called, hoping to set up an appointment for the following morning. It turned out that he was tied up with appointments all day. When I told him it was regarding Milo Getz, Terry invited me to come right over instead. I promised to be there in fifteen minutes.

I insisted upon loading the dishwasher before I left. It was the least I could do. I knew Crooked Branch Vineyards was a half kilometer south of Butterface Wines, barely ten minutes up Naramata Road from Mom's house. I had time.

A middle-aged couple were clearing tables in the tasting room when I arrived. I'd passed half a dozen guests on my way from the parking area, each with one or two bottles in hand. One of the women had been wearing an Aurora concert t-shirt.

Terry waved me inside the glass and timber structure. The place looked new. The dark brown leather chairs contrasted the cream tile floors perfectly. It was a blend of modern design and rustic comfort. I liked it. My eye was drawn to the largest of the photos hanging on the back wall. In it, the same couple, the Martin's obviously, plus Milo and Mavis were sharing a toast. There were smiles all around. Despite a wineglass in his hand, I spotted an open beer bottle on the counter, not far from the singer. That aligned with what Mavis had told me about him.

"This is very impressive," I said, as I stepped into the center of the building.

"Thank you," the woman responded. "We're happy with the way it turned out."

"Hi Reggie," the man stepped forward. "I'm Terry Martin and this is my wife, Ivy."

I shook both their hands, noting that Terry stood a little above six feet. He had thick shoulders and arms and appeared to be more than strong enough to lift 180 lbs.

"Thank you for meeting with me," I told them.

"If there is anything we can do to help…" Ivy said. Then she nodded at her husband. "You two have a seat, I'll finish tidying up."

"Thanks Dear," Terry kissed his diminutive spouse on the top of her head, before guiding me to the nearest chairs. "What would you like to know?"

"I understand that you were the last person to leave the party the night Milo died."

"Yes, I guess that's right," Terry said, his forehead wrinkling. "After everyone else left, Milo took Ross Gregory and me to see the new equipment he'd recently purchased. Ross owned the vineyard before he sold it to Milo."

"I'd heard that from someone," I mentioned.

"Used to be 'Gregory Estates Winery' before it became 'Butterface'," Ivy added, carrying a couple of half-filled wine glasses our way. The salmon-colored liquid looked cheerful as it danced inside the crystal-clear glass. We both thanked her as she headed back to continue wiping off the long cedar bar.

"Cheers," Terry said, raising his glass. I clinked mine lightly against it and then took a sip of the chilled wine. I expected sweet, but it was dry and refreshing. I picked up touches of oak and a hint of apricot.

"Very nice," I commented.

"Thank you," Terry replied. "This Rose' is our best seller."

"I can see why," I said. "This would be a perfect choice for sitting on the patio, watching the sun set."

"Yes it would," Ivy agreed. "It's also a great wine for a simple picnic of bread and cheese."

"It pairs very well with Gouda and Havarti," Terry said.

"Or my personal favorite," Ivy turned to us and smacked her lips, "aged camembert on crisp flat bread."

"Ooh, that does sound good," I agreed, before savoring another sip. I suddenly imagined Alan and I sitting peacefully on a blanket above the marina watching the boats come and go. Almost reluctantly, I steered the conversation back toward work. "You were telling me about 'Gregory Wine Estate' becoming 'Butterface'."

"Oh yes. We were quite surprised when Ross sold the place," Terry told me.

"That is until we heard rumors of the purchase price," Ivy said over her shoulder.

"Even still," Terry said. "He'd worked so hard to develop a very good selection of wines, some of them award winners. His Malbec won a national award. That was in 2004 wasn't it, hon?"

"That's right," Ivy confirmed, "and his Cabernet won Best in Region the year before that."

"His new winery over in Summerland," Terry said, "is starting to produce some very good wines."

"How did he feel about the new vineyard name and wines that 'Butterface' produced?" I asked, to keep the information rolling. I needn't have bothered. These two had lots to say. As they continued, I made a mental note to add Ross Gregory to my suspect list.

"Like the rest of us, he hated it," Ivy said, joining us.

"Wasn't much he could do about it," Terry told me. "Milo paid him twice what his place was worth. Plus, he let Ross keep the Gregory Estate label and the entire inventory."

"Was that unusual?"

"Well, yes," Terry said. "Once you've won some big awards, the label itself can be quite valuable, but Milo didn't want it. Of course, we would soon learn that he had big plans for his own label."

"If someone ever made us that kind of offer, we'd be so *out ah here*," Ivy laughed. I couldn't help but like the woman. There was a happy-go-lucky charm about her.

"Mavis and Milo spared no expense modernizing the place," Terry continued.

"New house, new buildings, new equipment," Ivy added. "I heard that Leslie, Mrs. Gregory, cried when she saw her house was gone. She'd been against selling the place, but the big bucks had already gotten to her husband."

"The house and buildings hadn't bothered Ross, so much. But when he found out they'd torn out his precious Malbec vines..." Terry's voice trailed off.

"You'd have thought he'd lost his first born," Ivy finished the thought for him.

"He'd been so proud of those grapes," Terry added. "Imported the seeds from the south of France."

In my mental notebook, I underlined Ross Gregory's name and added Leslie's.

"It really was a shame, they had twenty to thirty good producing years left in them," Ivy said, shaking her head. "We thought the Getz's were crazy at the time."

"But it turns out," Terry added, "Mavis is a talented grower and she had other ideas for that field. The matured vines there now are truly a thing of beauty."

"I heard that there was a coalition of sorts trying to ban Butterface Wines from the store shelves," I pointed out. "Was Mr. Gregory a part of that?"

"Yes, but so were we," Ivy admitted.

"We were more than a part of it, I'm ashamed to say," Terry said frowning. "I spearheaded the whole thing."

"You did?" I already knew that, but didn't let on.

"Oh yes," Terry freely stated. "I could understand it when he renamed the winery 'Butterface' after his most successful album." He put his hand up just as his wife was about to lodge a protest. "I didn't like it, but I understood. However, when I learned that he was calling his new offerings 'Zipper Ripper Red' and 'Bleached Blonde White' I about hit the roof. I thought Milo was making a mockery of the Okanagan wine industry."

"There was more to it than that, my dear," Ivy prodded. She scooched into her chair, getting comfortable. She had a smirk on her full lips and a twinkle in her dark brown eyes.

"Okay," Terry admitted. "I hated Milo Getz before any of that, before I ever met the man."

"Why?" I had to ask.

"The day after he bought the winery next door, he stole my vintner."

"Roman Angelo used to work for you?"

Terry nodded. "I just couldn't match the salary he'd been offered. I don't blame Roman for going, but it took me five years to find a winemaker half as good as he was -- still is. I hoped that if I put Butterface out of business Roman would come crawling back."

"What changed?"

"Nothing, I'd take him back in a heartbeat."

"I think she means, when did you stop hating Milo, Honeybunch?" Ivy chuckled.

"Oh yes, I was getting to that." Terry shrugged. "When I did finally sit down with him, Milo was nothing like I'd imagined. I found him to be both engaging and much to my surprise, very committed to promoting the wine industry."

"And?" Ivy pushed.

"And within a year of Butterface wines hitting the shelves we discovered that the sales of our own wines had increased by about five percent at the retail level. However, the big change for us was with tastings and 'in house' sales. They were up almost fifteen percent."

"That was our first truly profitable year," Ivy added.

"Yes, and the tasting traffic has substantially increased every year since," Terry pointed out.

"Our new wine shack is a direct result of Butterface being right next door," Ivy said. "The 'walk in' traffic keeps increasing due mainly to Milo."

"Every winemaker on the Naramata benches has benefited from the increased interest. Hell, every maker and grower in

Canada has benefited to some degree," Terry explained. "Butterface Wines added a younger demographic to our consumer base. Butterface got the millennials drinking wine."

"And the coalition?" I asked.

"Died out pretty quickly once everyone's sales began to increase," Ivy chuckled before taking a sip of wine.

"Milo quickly became one of the most influential ambassadors for Okanagan wines in the country," Terry said.

"Who'd have guessed that would happen?" I pondered. We all sat in silence for a few seconds. "You mentioned that Milo wanted to show you and Mr. Gregory some new equipment."

"He does have a new labelling machine, but that was just a ruse to get away from the stragglers at the party," Terry laughed. "He brought us down there so he could have a beer. Ross and I had some scotch that Milo kept down there, as well."

"What about those big new barrels?" I asked, remembering that they'd looked new.

"They were pretty hard to miss, eh? Ross asked Milo about them," Terry stated, then shrugged his shoulders. "We knew the new wine was in them, but Milo wouldn't talk about it."

"It was a secret but Mavis had confided in me that Butterface planned to start adding fine wines to the label. She and Roman had produced something special to launch the new line," Ivy informed me. "They are just about ready to start bottling the first of it."

"Have you heard of Coal River Wines?" Terry asked.

"No, I don't think so," I answered. I couldn't even recall any rivers by that name in the valley.

"They're an Australian wine maker," Terry said, but before he could explain further Ivy interrupted him.

"Tasmanian, actually," Ivy corrected her husband. "Mavis is always sure to make that distinction."

"Yes, she does. Forgive me, they are a Tasmanian wine maker," Terry chuckled. "Anyway, her family has been operating Coal River Wines for three generations. They produce some excellent whites."

"They make a truly wonderful Riesling," Ivy added.

"And if you like sparkling wines, they bottle a couple of very good ones," Terry told me. "Their reds, unfortunately, mediocre at best."

"Reds have always been a challenge for that region," Ivy pointed out. "When her parents came to visit shortly after Mavis and Milo moved here, her father wept at the sight of some of their hillside vines. The soil, the climate and the angle of the sun all combine for perfect growing conditions here. I think that's when Mavis decided she owed it to her family to produce some high-quality reds."

"Not that Zipper Ripper isn't a good wine," Terry said. "Quite the contrary, it is actually one of the best blended reds around and, in my opinion, Bleached Blonde White is the best blended white in Western Canada."

"People don't give their wines much credit because of the names, but every year they are consistently good," Ivy pointed out.

"Mavis is an excellent grower and Roman really is the best vintner in the valley." Terry got a tear in his eye before raising his glass. "And Milo put us on the map, may he be rocking out with Hendrix and Morrison right now."

"Here, here," Ivy and I joined in with the toast.

After a refill and another half hour of chatting with the Martins, I found out that they had legitimate concerns that once the renewed interest in Milo's life and death cooled off sales would drop. He had been an effective promoter and that would leave a void not easily filled. I also got the impression that they would genuinely miss Milo, their neighbor and friend.

Terry confirmed that he and Ross Gregory had been the last guests to go home the night of the party. Ivy said that Ross had been stunned when he learned the large quantities of wine Butterface sold. Terry already had a pretty good idea how successful the operation was, since he'd sold some of his crop to Butterface Wines, as had several other growers on the bench. Plus, Ivy informed me, Mavis and Milo had been quietly buying up land over the years and now produced grapes on more than a hundred-fifty acres. I'd asked if any of the sellers might hold a grudge, but to Terry's knowledge Milo had always paid fair market value or higher.

Terry told me that Ross had pestered Milo for a sample of the new wine all evening and night long, but Milo refused, telling him he'd have wait like everyone else. Ross hadn't been happy about it.

Terry confirmed that he and Ross had left at the same time the night Milo died. Ross had driven after assuring both Terry and Milo that he was capable. Ivy had driven home earlier, leaving her husband to walk since their house was barely a quarter mile away, as the crow flies. Ross had insisted on giving him a ride. The only oddity of note: he remembered seeing the barn lights go off and then turn back on just before he crawled into bed, perhaps a half hour after he'd gotten home.

As he walked me back to my car, Terry pointed across the field that separated Crooked Branch Vineyards and Butterface Wines. The big barn structure was clearly visible in the distance.

Once I got back to Betsy I transferred my mental notes to paper, Mr. and Mrs. Gregory each got a star beside their names.

After visiting with the Martins I'd pretty much scratched them off as suspects, though I'd learned over the years never to rule out anyone completely. They were still on the list, but no stars. It had been illuminating to learn that Milo's brand and marketing efforts had brought profits to the whole Okanagan wine industry. Though that didn't mean the other wineries and vineyards were off the hook as suspects. Rivalry and jealousy were strong motives. I mentally prepared myself to speak with each and every one of them. Sometimes you had to beat the bushes, or vines in this case, to get a clue to drop. I've never waited for clues to fall into my lap, I like to dig for them. Sometimes all it takes is a furtive glance or the tiniest slip of the tongue to break open a case.

The Martins had confirmed that Milo didn't drink wine or get involved with the production process. When I'd asked about

Milo's fear of heights, neither knew anything about it. Though, Terry couldn't recall ever seeing his neighbor on a ladder.

The barn lights going off and back on was curious. Plus, I had to wonder, if Milo had been alone in the barn when the 'so called' accident occurred, who had turned out the lights? Ernesto, the worker who discovered Milo's body, had clearly remembered turning on the barn lights when he arrived that morning. Someone else had been in the barn. I didn't know who, yet. I would keep looking until I found out.

CHAPTER 8

I still had no actual proof that Milo Getz had been murdered. His death had already been ruled as accidental by Detective Hannah Buckley and the PPD based on the coroner's report. She'd called me right after her press conference. Both Mavis Getz and my gut believed otherwise.

I glanced at my watch as I arrived back at the office, using my private entrance to avoid the inevitable disdainful glance from Mrs. Litmus. Four-thirty. The day was pretty much shot. For me it had been quite productive. I had a promising lead on Faux Jennifer. At lunchtime I'd squeezed in a photo session with Alan and took him to Whitespot for a burger, then slipped home to upload his new profile to the 'Rural Minglers' dating site. Plus, I now had a homicide investigation to solve.

Additionally, I'd spent a couple of hours trying to find a witness for one of Erika's impending cases. A homeless man, known in these parts as Jamaica or Jamaica John for his wild cornrowed looking hair, had witnessed a hit and run. Erika's client, a middle-aged woman, suffered a broken leg and pelvis. The owner of a large white late model pickup truck had raced through the intersection at Eckert and Main, while on his phone, clipping the poor woman, who was knocked backward onto the sidewalk. The driver stopped, got out of the truck, looked at the unconscious woman, then around to see if anyone was watching, jumped back in his truck and sped away. Jamaica John, I discovered was actually named William Hardy, thirty-eight years of age, formerly of Hamilton, Ontario, John had witnessed the entire event while raiding the dumpster of the nearby restaurant, Tequila Vallarta. The man had several priors for possession of illegal substances and vagrancy. He got a very good look at the driver. He'd reported what he'd seen to the responding officer, then disappeared. Based on his description, the police had charged a credible suspect, but had lost their witness.

This is when I got involved. After questioning several quite cooperative homeless folks, I was reasonably certain our witness had left Penticton. Hopefully, he was still somewhere in the Okanagan. If he'd gone to the coast he'd be harder to track down. I suspected that Kelowna or Vernon were more likely destinations.

I turned on my computer. FJ hadn't responded to Alan's 'cowpoke', yet. I'd continued my search for about an hour, on other dating sites, then headed for home.

The wind on my face felt good, so I rode right past Cambie onto Lower Bench Road. I decided to stop in and see how Mavis was doing despite her assurance she'd be alright. I hadn't been back to the Butterface Winery since the morning Milo had been discovered. It had been almost a week.

Speculation over his death had nearly consumed the Canadian airwaves until the coroner and PPD had officially ruled it an accident. 'Two Bagger' had become the number one requested song in the country since Milo's death; however, right now I had an Alannah Myles' song stuck in my head. I probably looked like a crazy person belting out the tune as I scootered along, but I didn't care.

"Black velvet with that slow southern style,
A new religion that will bring you to your knees,

Black velvet if you... Holy crap!" I pulled off to the side of the road and stared.

Mounds of flowers, teddy bears and dolls with paper bags covering their heads, were piled at least two meters high, adorning each side of the closed metal gate guarding the Butterface winery. Some of it had spilled over the fence onto the grounds inside. I guess Milo and his music had touched a lot of people. His memorial service had been yesterday. Family only, plus his band mates-- who, according to a local radio source -- Milo considered to be his real family.

I finally twisted the throttle, rolled up to the keypad podium and pressed the buzzer.

"The tasting room is closed, please come back tomorrow." I recognized Roman's voice.

"Roman, this is Reggie Swann," I shouted at the speaker, leaning as far to my left as I dared on Betsy. The gate immediately began to swing open. "Thank you."

The last time I saw the Butterface vintner he'd been heading up to the house to console the grieving widow. As I pulled up to the house, I wondered if there was something more than a love of grapes shared between Roman and Mavis.

Roman answered the door. He looked quite different in casual dress. I guess I did, too. He didn't remember me from the crime scene. I couldn't blame him. I'd been one of many and mostly in the background.

"Miss Swann?"

I heard soft laughter from deeper inside the house.

"Yes, please call me Reggie," I said, shaking his offered hand.

"I'm Roman," he responded, smiling warmly. "Mavis seems very pleased that you are here. Come this way."

I slipped out of my shoes and followed him down a corridor, past the living room. The floors were natural maple. I knew because I'd spent the better part of a week trying to decide what material to put in my suite. I'd almost chosen a flooring similar to this one, but got a great deal on an engineered Birch with a cinnamon stain. I hoped it would look half as good after the installation as this floor.

I'd expected to see gold records plastering the walls. Didn't spot a single one. The décor was very attractive but nothing indicated that a rock legend had lived here.

I noted the pleasant aroma of burning wood as we approached a room at the back of the house. A large floor-to-ceiling granite fireplace dominated the family room, where we joined Mavis and a very pregnant woman sitting on the floor between it and a tan leather sectional.

"Thank you for dropping by, Reggie." Mavis stood, steadying herself with the arm of the sofa before embracing me like an old friend. "This is Michelle, Roman's wife and my dearest friend."

"Hello Reggie," she said, reaching her hand upward. Michelle was one of those people who if you looked at their features individually you would think how unfortunate. Her nose was narrow and long, her eyes positioned a little too close together, the lips were pencil thin, but her infectious smile pulled everything together beautifully. One glance at Michelle told me she was a glass-half-full kind of person, who smiled most of the time.

"Hi Michelle, it's nice to meet you," I said, leaning down to shake her hand.

"Sorry," Michelle laughed, "now that I'm down here, I may need a crane to get me back on my feet."

I noticed all three of the beverages present were also sitting on the floor. Two large stemless wine glasses and an insulated tumbler in front of Michelle. There was also a large crystal decanter with perhaps a couple of glasses of dark red wine left in it on the fireplace mantel near Mavis.

Mavis grabbed my hand and towed me forward and down to Michelle's level. "Join us, you can help come up with a name for the newest member of our family."

"Boy or girl?" I asked, glancing over at Michelle.

"Pinot Noir," Mavis giggled, while the other two faces turned serious. "Oops, I've spilled the beans. Reggie, you can keep a secret, can't you?"

"Is this about the new wine you're releasing?" I asked, guessing from her demeanor that Mavis had already consumed a few glasses of wine.

"How do you know about that?" Roman asked.

"She is a bloody gumshoe," Mavis retorted before I could respond, as if being a PI meant that I knew everything. I wish.

"I won't say a word about it to anyone, I promise."

"There you see," Mavis said. "No harm, no foul." Roman and Michelle visibly relaxed. She returned her gaze to me. "I take it that you've started the investigation?"

"Yes," I said reluctantly, feeling distress at her asking the question in front of Roman, one of my prime suspects.

"We know that Mavis hired you," Michelle stated. "We encouraged it."

"Have you learned anything?" Roman asked.

"I'm just getting started," I stammered uncomfortably.

"It's okay, Reggie," Mavis said, nodding her approval. "You can speak freely in front of Roman and Mishie. They are my dearest friends. We're all in this together."

"Alright." I cleared my throat. "As I said, I'm only just getting started. So far, I've only spoken with the Martins and a few other nearby vineyard owners."

"You found out about the new release from Ivy," Roman said, looking at Mavis, who shrugged.

"Terry and Ivy are the salt of the earth, they had nothing to do with Milo's death," Mavis interjected.

"I don't think so either," I confirmed. "But Terry was one of the last people to..."

"You should talk to that bitch, Rosemary Eberle," Michelle interrupted. "Her and her husband, Damien Eberle, own Fallen Leaf Wines, north of here about a kilometer. She went on and on, at the party last week, about how our sample prices are too low. She complained that too many tourists end their tasting tour at Butterface. We only have two wines to try. It isn't our fault if people have seconds or thirds."

"Rosemary isn't a bitch, Sweetheart," Roman said. "She has a legitimate concern, one we should probably address."

"Legitimate concern or not," Michelle whispered to me, "she is a bitch."

I made a mental note to speak to the Eberles.

"As far as the investigation is concerned, it is too early to draw any conclusions," I sounded like I was making an official statement to the press, but in this case, it was true. "Tell me about the new wine."

"The first of the new wines we're adding to the label is a Pinot Noir," Roman explained. "We've been keeping this a secret until the big release next month."

"Nobody knows?"

"Just us three and a handful of trusted staff," Roman said. "Plus, the Martins and now you."

"Ross Gregory is also aware of the new wine," I added.

"I wonder how he found out about it?" Roman said, squinting accusingly at Mavis.

"Why are you staring at me?" Mavis giggled again. "I guess it is possible I accidentally mentioned our new wine during coffee one morning."

"I never understood the connection between the two of you," Roman said.

"What's to understand," Mavis shrugged. "We both grow grapes..."

"Anyway," Michelle interjected, "we've been trying, rather unsuccessfully I might add, to come up with a name for the new wine. We have to get the labels ordered." She then patted her bulging tummy and looked over at her husband. "Roman and I have decided to name our son-to-be, Emilio."

"Emilio, that's a great name," I said, then remembered something I'd heard recently. "You're naming him after Milo." Milo had been born Emilio Andrew Getz. Apparently, his mother had always called him Melo, but to his friends and then the rest of the world he'd become Milo. You can learn all kinds of trivia listening to the radio.

"He would have been so honored and pleased," Mavis added softly, her giggles replaced by a sad smile. "Thank you."

"You're welcome," Michelle said.

Mavis pushed away a threatening tear and then threw her shoulders back and raised her head high flashing a genuine smile.

"Roman, don't be such a wanker," Mavis scolded him, in a good-natured way. "Offer our guest a beverage."

"Of course, forgive me Reggie," Roman laughed. "What can I get you to drink? Some of us are having wine and one of us -- root beer." He smirked down at Michelle before returning his gaze to me.

"Wine please."

"Good girl." Mavis smiled, while Roman left the room. "You can help us with the name."

"I doubt I'll be any help," I said. "I'm not very creative."

"You can't do any worse than us," Roman laughed, returning with a glass which he passed to Mavis.

"We honestly don't know what to call the new family of finer wines." Mavis shrugged and poured some wine from the decanter in front of her and then handed the glass to me. "We're starting with the Pinot Noir and plan to add two more by the end of next year, and another three the following year."

"Wow, that sounds very impressive," I said.

"It would be," Mavis laughed. "But we can't launch anything without a name."

"Milo was the idea guy in our group," Michelle told me.

"We're pretty sure he'd already chosen a name and designed a label," Mavis informed me while Roman poured some wine from the decanter, before emptying the rest into her glass. "But he kept it a secret, even from us."

"He had me order special bottles," Roman said, "but wouldn't offer a hint about the name."

"He loved naming the wines and designing the labels," Michelle said. "He had quite the sense of humor and, of course, a flair for the dramatic."

"And you couldn't argue with his success," Roman said. "Bleached Blonde is the best-selling white in the whole country."

"Here, here," Michelle said, raising her glass.

"Here, here," we all responded.

I took a sip. This was not Zipper Ripper, as I'd assumed. I lifted the glass to my nose and breathed in deeply, while I slowly experienced the myriad of distinct flavors still lingering on my tongue. Naturally, I realized, winemakers would drink excellent wines from around the world. I hadn't tasted a wine of this caliber before. It was obviously well beyond my budget. Probably French or a very good Napa. I savored another sip, until I suddenly felt all eyes upon me.

"This cannot be your new wine?" I challenged the smiling faces surrounding me.

"What do you think?" Mavis asked.

"You guys made this wine? Here in the Okanagan?"

"We did," Roman nodded proudly.

"It is exceptional – a whole concert of flavors exploded in my mouth at once."

"Crikey," Mavis exclaimed. "Stone the crows, I think we have a winner."

"Of course! Why hadn't we thought of that," Michelle said, glancing from her friend up to her husband and then over to me. "It works on every level!"

"What did I say?" I asked, totally confused.

"Concert," Michelle confirmed.

"For days we've been searching for just the right word that best describes the new wines, fits with the label's image, and is a tribute to Milo," Roman said. "And you just blurted it out."

"To Concert," Mavis lifted her glass towards the ceiling. "Butterface Wine's new offerings."

"Concert," Michelle and Roman chanted together, as they joined their glasses to hers. I followed suit.

"Concert wines, I love it," Mavis said. "The label could feature a picture of Milo and the band rocking out on stage."

"A whole series of photos from the concerts they performed around the world," Michelle suggested.

"That's a great idea. Fans could collect the complete set," Roman said. "It's not just a name, it's an entire marketing campaign."

"Six new wines, with perhaps six different labels each," Mavis continued the thought. "I think..." Her voice faltered, she took a breath then spoke again. "I think Milo would approve."

"I know he would," Michelle confirmed, then she reached over and took her friend's hand.

Mavis nodded as a tear rolled down her cheek, then turned to me and smiled. "You see Reggie, you're more creative than you give yourself credit for."

"It wasn't me," I confessed. "It was the wine. This truly is the most amazing wine I've ever tasted."

"Roman has really outdone himself," Mavis stated, holding her glass toward him.

"Only because I had the finest grapes in the whole valley to work with," Roman quickly acknowledged, then brought his glass to hers.

"And now we have the perfect name," Michelle added, her tumbler joining the others.

"Reggie, you're a part of this now." Mavis smiled at me and indicated that I should join in.

"Glad I could help," I said, pushing my glass forward, still not at all certain I'd actually done anything.

"To Milo and the new Concert family of wines," Roman toasted.

"Here, here," we joined in. This time I took in a proper mouthful of the delicious dark liquid.

Mavis excused herself. She returned a few minutes later carrying an armload of photo albums. We spent the next couple hours looking at and choosing our favorite concert shots of Milo and the band. Amongst laughter and tears Mavis explained where each image was taken, personal photos included. I saw another side of the intense rock star, who seemed to personify sex, drugs and rock 'n roll in the public eye. Out of the spotlight, Milo looked just like any other regular guy. Gone were the tight leather pants and the glittery shirt, in favor of jeans and a tee. The biggest difference though, was the hair. On stage, his trademark unruly hair surrounded his head like a shaggy living halo. In fact, much to the amusement of those present, I hadn't recognized the man with the slicked back hair standing next to Mavis in the first few photos.

I learned that the rock star preferred dinners with friends to parties with strangers. His 'real' life revolved around Mavis, the Toronto Maple Leafs, museums and reading. Milo had been a voracious reader. I don't know why that surprised me, and I'd never have guessed museums and a love of history in a million years. The Maple Leafs, for sure, but museums...

CHAPTER 9

Throughout the evening Roman, Mavis and Michelle behaved like siblings. I could feel the love and the loss they all shared. I could tell that the four of them had become one big happy family. It was a great relief to know that Mavis wasn't grieving alone.

I was surprised and pleased to learn that I would be able to afford this wine. At double the price of Butterface's first two wines, the new offerings would still be a bargain compared to other local wines. Coming from humble beginnings himself, Milo believed in keeping things affordable for all. He'd argued, throughout his music career, to keep concert prices down and often bought out entire rows of seats to give away to the less fortunate. This softer side of Milo was kept from the public, in favor of the more traditional and expected hard partying rocker dude persona.

I also discovered that Roman was more than an employee and a friend. A year earlier, Milo and Mavis made him a full third partner in the business. The Getz's had offered him part of the business years earlier, but he'd turned them down, preferring to wait until he had something more tangible to bring to the partnership. That had happened when he and his brother inherited twenty-eight acres of bench land. He bought his brother out and Butterface Winery added twenty-eight much needed fertile acres to its growing vineyards.

I'd already known that Roman was one of the top vintners in the valley and that Milo had become one of the region's best wine promoters, but when Roman made a joke about Mavis being the 'Grape Whisperer' I had to know more. He explained, in layman's terms, that for optimum flavor, the grapes must get just the right amount of water through their growth cycle. Too much watering was just as bad as too little. He swore that no one could judge watering as well as his partner. Mavis tried to shake it off, but Michelle insisted that she tell me the 'Jerara' story. After some coaxing, she finally relented.

"When I was five," Mavis closed her eyes and began reciting, "an aboriginal man from the mainland knocked on our door early one Sunday morning. Despite the man's rough appearance, my parents invited him in. The strange man refused the invitation, preferring to stay on the porch. He turned out to be a bushman from the Outback. He'd gone on walkabout, where he'd seen a vision of an island and a house that looked just like ours. It apparently took him months to find us, but without a doubt, Jerara -- that was his name, believed he was right where he should be. Jerara informed my father that he'd be with us as long as we needed him to be and then turned around and left the house. We all watched as he wandered into the nearby woods."

"Mysterious," I said, taking another sip.

"I just love this story," Michelle said, her smile wider than ever. "I've heard it a dozen times and it gives me chills every time."

"Each and every morning after that, Jerara would be waiting in the yard to go to out the vineyards with my father," Mavis continued. "He knew nothing about grapes or making wine, but he didn't get in Dad's way so my father tolerated the old man's presence. I often followed them around. Jerara loved to tease me and I loved the attention. Jerara didn't like enclosed places, so whenever Dad went inside the barns Jerara stayed outside. After a couple years…"

"Years?" I interrupted.

"Yes, years," Michelle confirmed.

"After a couple years, Jerara seemed like one of the family. I didn't know where he slept at night, but he was always there every morning. Warm or cold, Jerara always dressed the same. I never saw the man sweat or shiver. As he learned more about growing grapes our crops began to improve. My father said that Jerara seemed to know within minutes and millimeters when and how much it would rain. Dad started watering the vines accordingly."

Mavis smiled before continuing, her eyes seeing beyond us and through the walls. "I followed him around like a yearling joey. If I wasn't in school, I was hopping along at Jerara's heals. I mirrored everything he did. When he ran his fingers through the dirt or turned his face into the breeze, I did too. If he chewed on a leaf, I ate one. One morning Jerara looked up at the clouds and asked me if I thought it would rain that day. I knew it wouldn't rain for two more days and I told him so. He laughed, took me by the hands and twirled me around and around until we were dizzy. I didn't know when it had happened but somehow he'd passed his gift onto me. I'd just had my eleventh birthday."

Mavis paused, her smile flickered and drifted away.

"The very next morning, Jerara knocked on our house door, for only the second time, thanked my parents for their hospitality and said it was time for him to go home. I walked him to the edge of our property, where he told me I'd also been in his walkabout vision."

"Wow," I said. "And you can still predict when it will rain?"

"Nothing for the rest of the week, on this side of the lake." Mavis' smile returned. "They'll get 2-3 millimeters in Peachland tomorrow afternoon."

"You're kidding?"

"You can bank on it," Roman told me.

"Tell her the rest," Michelle urged.

"When I was in high school I wrote a report on the people that had most influenced me. Of course, Jerara was on the list. I did some research and discovered the meaning of his name." Mavis paused for dramatic effect. "In the aboriginal language Jerara means 'falling water'."

"Isn't that the coolest story you've ever heard?" Michelle asked.

"Wow, very cool," I admitted. "Makes me want to visit that part of the world."

"Really," Michelle agreed.

"I have something for you," Mavis told me, reaching for a bundled stack of papers sitting on a nearby coffee table. "These are the physical threats that Milo received in the last few years. Some by mail, some of them through the internet."

"Thank you," I said, noting she found them upsetting. My eyes must have revealed that I'd been surprised at the quantity.

"This is nothing. When I first met Milo, he got this many every week," Mavis stated. "He never took them seriously -- thought they were funny. He used to throw them all away. I know that one thing has nothing to do with the other, but after his fall he started keeping them."

She didn't need to say it out loud. I could see that was when Milo first figured out he was mortal like everyone else. Maybe, that's also when Mavis realized the same thing. Tears started to form in her eyes. I cupped her hands in mine, for a couple of seconds, before taking the paper from her. "Keeping them was very smart. These may help."

"Anyone need more wine or root beer?" Roman asked, relieving the tension that filled the room.

"Please," Mavis laughed, wiping away some tears with a finger. Lighter conversation resumed.

Before I went home, Roman took me up to the tasting room. Now I knew where all Milo's gold records were being displayed, along with several guitars, costumes and other memorabilia. During my private tour Roman also showed the area where the small raised stage had been before Milo's accident. They'd torn it out and redone the area level to the floor. Even the tall stool he'd sat on had been replaced with a shorter one that allowed his feet to stay grounded.

"Milo had a rare gift," Roman shared with me, as he reverently touched the top of the guitar propped next to the stool. "He connected with people. Within seconds of meeting him, people felt a genuine bond to him. A couple times each day, Milo popped in for a 'surprise' meet and greet. He would chat and joke around with everyone present, buy a round of samples and then grab one of his guitars and perform a few songs. I've been present during more than a hundred of these impromptu visits and every one of them felt like Milo was sharing something very special with his new friends."

"I'm sorry that I never got the chance to meet him." Looking around the beautiful room, I could imagine how intimate and amazing a live performance by the rock legend would have been.

"He never seemed to tire of signing labels or posing for selfies," Roman explained. "With Milo present, 'in the house' sales jumped exponentially. No one could sell wine like Milo Getz."

"Do you know of anybody who would want to hurt Milo?"

"Not really," Roman said after a few seconds of thought. "Some of the other growers and producers might be a little jealous of the amount of business we do, but Milo has been good for everyone's sales."

"What about the woman Michelle mentioned?" I asked.

"Rosemary Eberle?" He enquired, then continued after I nodded. "I guess you could say she's a strong-willed woman, but she and her husband are good people. I get along just fine with Damien. I understand how frustrating it must be for them to see how much traffic we get here, only to watch most of it turn around and head back toward Penticton."

"Frustrating enough to kill?"

"No," Roman said firmly, then thought for a few seconds. "Well, I don't believe so."

"Were the Eberles here the night of the party?"

"Yes, but they left early," Roman said, then hesitated as if trying to decide whether to tell me something.

"What is it?" I prodded.

"Shortly before they left I did see Rosemary having a heated discussion with Milo, but I'm sure it was nothing. He hadn't mentioned it to me."

On my way in, I'd noticed the heavy locks on the doors and security cameras in all four upper corners of the large room. He explained that the impressive wall of windows, overlooking the lake, were made of Lexan, not glass. I was truly at a loss for words when Roman told me how valuable the guitars and other band memorabilia was. As we toured the room, looking at each photo, gold record, guitar and other sorted items all carefully arranged in chronological order, I realized that Milo had curated his very own museum.

After Michelle and Roman had confirmed Milo's fear of heights and then seeing the lowered stage area myself, I was certain that Milo hadn't climbed that ladder. Someone had staged his death to look like an accident. I felt more determined than ever to figure out who had done this.

Roman made me copies of the guest book pages, going back a couple of weeks, and provided copies of the security footage from the night of the party. I knew that Hannah and her team had already gone through most of this, but once the coroner ruled the death an accident the case had been quickly closed. A fresh, more determined set of eyes might spot something or someone that had been overlooked.

CHAPTER 10

I was just about back to Betsy, when my new phone buzzed in my pocket. The short buzz indicated an incoming text. I'd been reluctant to get a smart phone, but both Alan and Hannah had sung their virtues until I relented. While I was in prison, or as Mom likes to say 'while I was away' -- as if I'd been on an extended trip to Europe or somewhere pleasant – texting had become the preferred method for communication. For some reason, and I still wasn't quite there yet, people screened their incoming calls but usually responded to texts immediately. I pulled out the smaller-sized two-generation-old I-phone that I'd opted for. I tapped the dark screen and it lit up.

'Need to talk. Bad Tattoo Brewing. 15 minutes.' The text message was from Hannah.

'OK,' I replied, then pulled on my helmet. Pizza sounded pretty good to me after having only wine and a few potato chips all evening. Betsy wanted to exceed the posted speed limit a few times on the twisty road into town, but I kept her reigned in. I'd only had two glasses of the exquisite wine but didn't want to risk blowing into a breathalyzer.

I got there first and secured a corner table. I ordered a large 'Comfort Zone' pizza and a pitcher of ice water.

Hannah arrived just as our waiter brought the water. Hannah sat and immediately drank half a glass.

"Can I get you something else to drink?" the waiter asked Hannah.

"No thanks, water will do for now," she replied, surprising me. Normally, she had a beer after work.

"Thanks for meeting with me," she said, setting the glass down.

"Of course," I assured my best friend. "What's going on?"

"Miller is driving me crazy."

I figured she'd asked me here to vent about her new partner. Detective Quincy Miller was less than a year from retirement and forty years past his last original idea. I'd met him a few times. Nice enough fellow, though he seemed more like eighty-four than sixty-four. The man moved and spoke extremely slowly and if he'd ever had any imagination, he'd lost it somewhere. He'd told me the same story about his youngest grandchild losing one of his runners, while playing hide and seek, each time I'd chatted with him. They'd found the boy, but never did find his sneaker.

"How he ever made detective, I'll never know." Hannah rolled her eyes. "Three times today, during a suspect interview, I finished his sentences."

"No, you didn't," I laughed.

"I couldn't help myself," Hannah snorted. "It was just like the sloth scene from 'Zootopia'."

"I loved that movie." Alan and I had rented it a couple of weeks earlier. Well, to be honest, I'd picked it out as a joke. Alan liked hard-boiled action adventures like the 'Die Hard' movies. However, even he'd enjoyed it. I wouldn't be surprised if he added it to his extensive video collection. "You working on anything interesting?"

"I wish... vandalism. Someone spray painted unpleasant messages on half a dozen cars parked on the east end of Edmonton Avenue last Saturday night."

"Kids?"

"Maybe a teen," Hannah said with some doubt in her voice. "The artwork is pretty impressive. Whoever did it has some skill. I have some pictures with me."

The pizza arrived as Hannah passed them over to me. My stomach demanded that I tear into it, but I already had a hand full of photos, so I resisted the urge and looked them over.

Hannah was right about the skill level of the artist. I'd never seen the word slut written so beautifully before. Across the side of a sporty-looking Mazda, the 'i's in the words 'pencil dick' were finely detailed parts of the male anatomy. In a couple of the pictures, I could see that the artist had skipped several cars between those he'd painted. Two of the cars vandalized had been in driveways, the other four parked on the street.

"I see what you mean," I said, handing the photos back with the two driveway cars on top and finally getting my hands on a slice. "I'm thinking one or both of these two cars may have been the original targets."

"I do too, but Miller believes it was just some graffiti artist who got bored with tagging trains," Hannah said, already scooping up a second pizza wedge. I evidently wasn't the only hungry person at the table. "Oh man, this is good. I didn't realize how hungry I was until I sat down."

I nodded, groaning with agreement, unable to speak. My mouth filled with the uniquely wonderful combination of ham, apples, tomato sauce and cheese. This was the second time I'd had this pizza. I'd been skeptical the first time, but Mom had insisted. I'd loved it then, but it had been my first restaurant pizza in almost a decade and I didn't have much to compare it to at that time. I'd had several offerings from other pizza shops since then, but none that I liked as well as that first bite from here. I hoped it would taste as good as I remembered. It did not disappoint. I don't know why the combination of toppings surprised me again. Apples and cheese go great together, so do ham and cheese. Yet, I'd never seen this combination before, anywhere else. I smiled at Hannah and took another bite.

"You catch your identity thief yet?" Hannah asked.

"I think I may have a lead on her," I said. Then told her all about the trap I'd set using Alan's picture and a fake profile. We shared a few laughs over some of the women who'd responded. I was about to admit to her about looking into Milo's death, despite the fact that she and the PPD had ruled it an accident, when she completely surprised me with news of her own.

"The real reason I wanted to talk to you is..." Hannah told me, getting a serious look on her face. "...to prepare you for your upcoming duties as a Godmother."

"A Godmother? How?"

"Well, Reggie, when a man and a woman love each other..." Hannah laughed at me.

"You're pregnant?" I asked, still wrapping my head around the news.

"Got the results back this morning," Hannah confirmed. "Six weeks."

"Oh my God, this is wonderful news." I stared into her eyes to confirm that she was happy about it. Her huge smile told me she was. I wrapped my arms around my best friend and gave her a mighty squeeze. "Congratulations, Hannah! I'm so happy for you."

"Thank you," she said, her face beaming. "You're the first person I've told, besides Danny, of course."

"He must be just thrilled."

"Over the moon," Hannah said. "We talked it over and we want you and Alan to be the Godparents."

"I, we'd be honored," I answered for both of us, without any qualms. Alan and Danny really hit it off. Once the four of us began doing things together they'd been almost inseparable. The three of them could talk and argue about football and hockey for hours, while I soaked in an audio highlight reel of all the great plays and games I'd missed. For the past six months, at least every other weekend, the four of us had hiked, biked, done wine tastings, gone to hockey games or movies or just hung out together. "Wow, a baby, that is amazing."

"No beer or wine for me for a while," Hannah said, as a platter of alcoholic beverages wafted past us.

"Small price to pay," I assured her.

"Easy for you to say," she countered, then laughed. "I know, I know."

"Hannah, I have something to tell you, too."

"You're not?" She glanced down at my stomach.

"No, I'm definitely not having a baby," I strongly denied, though the thought of having a baby of my own wasn't a new one. In prison, I'd been both grateful for and regretful of not having children. I'd been grateful they wouldn't have to see me in a place like that. At the same time, regretful I'd likely never get to experience motherhood. Oh, Mom had done her best to make certain I'd never give up hope of being released, but as the months and years dragged by the doubts had crept in. I couldn't deny the overwhelming jealousy I'd felt after learning that Trent had a baby with his new wife.

I still had time, I reminded myself. Alan was great. In fact, he was perfect. He'd said the 'L' word to me more than once. I loved him, too, but couldn't bring myself to verbalize it. Mom adored him from the start, but something held me back. I knew what it was. Deep down I was afraid that if I let him into my heart, he'd leave like all the other important men in my life had.

"What is it?" Hannah asked, noticing the odd look on my face.

As truly happy as I was for Hannah and Danny, I was also anxious to change the subject. I wasn't sure how Hannah would feel about me looking into a case she'd already closed. I didn't have very many close friends and couldn't afford to lose my bestie.

"I'm looking into the death of Milo Getz," I spurted out. Hannah got very serious. My stomach knotted. Oh, no. She'd been the lead investigator on his case and I'd just insulted her abilities as a detective. So much for being a Godmother.

"I'm happy to hear you say that."

"Mavis Getz hired me; she believes her husband was murdered," I offered as an excuse, as my mind unscrambled her words. "Wait, so you're not upset?" I felt so relieved.

"Just the opposite, girlfriend. We closed that case far too quickly for my liking," Hannah confided. "There were some anomalies I wanted to address, but when the coroner ruled his death accidental there was nothing I could do. The case was closed and I was reassigned."

"The vandalism over on Skaha Road?" A few nights earlier, I'd learned from Mom, someone or several someones had smashed several storefront windows, stripped the clothes off a bunch of mannequins and laid them out in suggestive positions all over the street.

"Yup," Hannah chuckled. "It was quite educational. I learned a few new positions."

"You? I don't believe that for a second."

"There was this one," Hannah leaned forward and whispered. "Danny and I tried it last night, where you arch your back and grab your right ankle with your left hand..."

I held up my hand and shook my head, to stop her. "Ooh, not while we're eating. In fact, not ever."

"I'm just yanking your chain, Swann," Hannah laughed. "Geez, you should have seen your face. Fifty shades of red. You're so easy."

"I should have known that you hadn't learned any new positions."

"Of course not." We giggled like teenagers. I always end up laughing out loud when I'm with Hannah. It feels good after so many years without joy. I'd lost hope of ever having evenings like this again.

As we finished the pizza, our chatting turned more serious. We went over the oddities at the Getz crime scene. Things like the half-wiped table and the fact that lights had been turned off. Small things that didn't shout murder. But who would climb a ladder in the dark? Though, Hannah pointed out the possibility that there could be a flashlight at the bottom of the tank. I hadn't thought of that. I told her about Milo's extreme fear of heights, citing how he would no longer perform on a raised stage or even climb the stairs in his own house. I shared my earlier conversations with the Martins, Roman, the also pregnant Michelle and Mavis. From her interviews with Roman and other Butterface employees, Hannah already knew about their plans to release a new series of fine wines. Without going into the specifics of type or release date I shared the story of how I'd come up with the secret name for the new wine. Despite the lack of detail, Hannah seemed to find my tale hilarious. After a few more laughs we got back to the subject of my new investigation. Since Milo's previous wine labels had angered most of the winemakers and his music had offended at least half the country's population, we agreed that the suspect pool was vast.

Hannah offered her assistance in an unofficial capacity. She took home the stack of threats that Mavis had provided. The team was back together. I knew I'd have to do most of the heavy lifting, but it was reassuring to have Hannah there in my corner for support.

Hannah is having a baby! A cute, cuddly baby...

CHAPTER 11

It was after ten by the time I got home. A note on the fridge informed me that Mom was out with friends and my contractor wanted to speak with me. It wasn't too late to call Buck, but I wasn't in the mood for any bad news. I wasn't even tempted to go down to the basement to check on the progress. He and the renovation could wait until the morning.

I sat down at the kitchen table, cradled my face in my hands and wept for my unborn children. I was thrilled for Hannah and Danny, but at the same time her news had reminded me that I didn't have the girl and boy I'd expected to have by now. If my life had gone as planned, Andrea or Dylan would have been in first grade by now, with their little sister or brother in pre-school. It didn't help with my mood to think about Trent and his new wife going through all the things I'd missed, while sitting alone in my cell -- first smile, first word, first step. After the tears relented, I searched the cupboards looking for some chocolate. I finally found a bag of semi-sweet baking chips hiding behind a box of Chia seeds. Mom's pantry was filled with ancient grains and strange seeds. Another trend that happened while I was incarcerated. I poured a large mound of chocolate chips onto a napkin and carried the treasure up to my room.

The world had changed while I was away. For better, for worse, I was still on the fence. At least I had Alan. Since I'd been seeing him, my life had become joyful again. There was still time for an Andrea and a Dylan. *Don't get too ahead of yourself, Reggie...* I popped a couple chocolate morsels into my mouth and let them melt on my tongue. Plus, I had my work. It was true, I was not a cop anymore, but I was still an investigator. In some ways I actually liked being a private detective better. I did not miss the office politics or being told what cases to take or when to move on. After I'd been vindicated, Toronto PD had offered me my old job back. I loved being a homicide detective, but after some soul searching I'd opted to stay in Penticton and start a new life. So far, I hadn't regretted that decision.

I felt so relieved to be on the same page with Hannah. She wanted to help with Milo. Working a case with her was always better than without. We were unofficial partners. While at the restaurant she and I had looked through some of the threatening letters Milo had received. They were from all over the country and in a few cases from beyond our borders. There were also copies of digital correspondence from the Aurora website. The band and Butterface Winery had a social media presence, but Milo did not. He didn't do Facebook, Twitter or Instagram. Since Hannah had the resources of the police department at her disposal, I'd let her take the letters while I concentrated on the locals from the guest list. We planned to meet and compare our findings at the end of the week.

As I sat down at my old desk, I was reminded of all the homework I'd done right there during my high school days. I hadn't been much of a studier. I paid attention during class, most of the time, and did all the assignments. I remembered enough from doing that to get A's on the exams. Lois Baxter and I got similar marks all through school. She was a studier. She memorized facts and figures. She could tell you who, what, when, and where, but the why often eluded her. I'd especially loved the why. Always had. I think that's what makes me a good detective. Once I'd figured out the why, whether it was American History or a murder case, the rest makes sense to me.

I still didn't understand why Milo had been murdered, but I knew I'd eventually figure that out.

With Faux J, the why was money, mixed with the excitement of playing the game. I was closing in on her. Now calling herself Mary Beth Walker, I'd alerted the real Mary Beth, plus the authorities, and now I had only a day or two before Faux J would realize that her latest identity was blown, then she'd skip town again.

I flipped open my laptop and found 134 cowpokes waiting in my inbox. Instead of winks, nods or nudges, this site used cowpokes to signal interest. I had not expected such a large response to the profile I'd set up. Country boy Alan, whom I'd re-named Tom, did seem like a pretty good catch. Maybe I'd made him too good. Alan was better looking than FJs usual targets, but I'd picked one of the least flattering photos to combat this.

Unfortunately, I'd have to open each cowpoke to see who it was from. I popped a couple more chocolate morsels into my mouth and clicked the first response to my boyfriend. The profile of the 'I'd like to corral you, cowboy' girl turned out to be big eyed and even bigger chested. She definitely wasn't Faux J, so I clicked on the next cowpoke. 'Farmer's daughter' appeared to be quite naked underneath a skimpy pair of bibbed overalls. I'd probably been wise not telling Alan which sites I'd posted his profile onto.

Several morsels and profiles later the fingers of my right hand brushed across the empty napkin as my left index finger hovered above the mousepad. I glanced over and my eyes confirmed what my fingers already knew – no more chocolate morsels. I was too lazy to go downstairs to the kitchen and retrieve more.

"Come on, sister," I said, refocusing on the tedious task, "at least try to be original."

I stared at the fifteenth or sixteenth 'Hey Stud, I'd love to ride you hard and put you away wet,' message I'd come across already and I was barely half way through the cowpoke pile. I'd like to think most guys wouldn't respond to crap like this, but of course, many of them would. I wanted to skip these ones, but I had to be thorough. I double tapped on her profile. As I'd guessed this wasn't FJ, either. Christie May Oliver, however, liked cowboys, rodeos and skinny dipping. I could also tell from the full-length swimwear photo of her in the upper righthand corner of the screen that one of Christie May's other hobbies had been breast augmentation.

For just a moment, I wondered whether Alan had ever done any online dating. He'd been quite upfront about his love life. Alan had gone out with lots of women. I could understand that: the guy was single, good looking and he hadn't been locked away in a prison like some of us. Only twice had he had relationships that lasted more than a year. I had a long way to go to match Deirdre. She'd been the only multiple year woman in Alan's life. He'd been engaged to Deirdre. She'd been the life of the party, he'd told me. Everyone loved Deidre. She was smart and beautiful, but living with her had become a challenge. Saying the wrong thing or even looking at her the wrong way could set off an angry tirade that could last for days. He'd suspected his fiancé might be bi-polar, but she refused to see a doctor about it.

The day after their wedding invitations went out, she'd packed up and left without explanation. Alan said he'd loved Deidre and missed her for a long time, but had admitted feeling like a giant weight had been taken off his shoulders when he came home and found her gone. Deidre had offered Alan no explanation as to what had happened or why and after a while, he'd dropped the matter. A year later Deidre suddenly up and married someone else. She currently lived in Okanagan Falls, not even twenty minutes away. Now, when Alan ran into her socially, Deidre treated him like a dear old friend.

"Over time I came to realize that she did me a huge favor the day she left. Fun Deidre was a blast, but there was a dark side to her. There was no middle ground with her, she was up or she was down. I sometimes had the feeling I'd yet to see the darkest parts of her," he'd told me. "Instead, I met you and my life has never been better. You make me very happy, Reggie Swann."

I could tell by the way he spoke about Deidre that he still cared for her, probably always would. I understood completely. After all, I still harbored feelings for my ex, though I wished with all my heart that I didn't after what he'd done to me. At least Trent was thousands of kilometers away.

I'd looked at approximately twenty more profiles when a giant yawn reminded me how late the hour had gotten. It didn't look promising that I'd find Faux J amongst this group of desperate women. Eight more profiles to go and I'd hit the one hundred mark. I promised myself I'd stop then and do the rest in the morning.

On the ninety-eighth profile, my drooping eyes popped wide open. There was fake Jennifer, now fake Mary Beth, looking back at me. I recognized the eyes and mouth immediately. The cowpoke had read, 'You sound like someone I'd love to learn more about'. Since Mary Beth Walker had contacted me, well more accurately had contacted Tom, I had access to a more detailed profile. Mary Beth's likes also included: starry nights, wide open spaces, attending the Calgary Stampede and home cooked meals. Subtle, just like the profile image she'd posted of a perfectly wholesome girl next door. Unfortunately, there wasn't a street address or phone number listed, but she had mentioned enjoying Canmore since moving to the small city. Several of the more blatant country gals had suggested very intimate first dates. Mary Beth, playing it cool, suggested meeting for coffee or lunch. Her photos and profile page had been carefully planned. There was some cute playfulness mixed in with subtle depth that gave the impression of someone you'd be proud to introduce to friends and family.

"Gotcha," I said to myself, though I wasn't as confident as I sounded. Mary Beth would pull up stakes and catch the first stage coach out of town once she learned her newest identity had been compromised. I'd have to work fast. I'd need some help from my friends. I reached for my phone but froze, remembering that it was well after midnight. My mind raced with plans as I readied myself for bed.

CHAPTER 12

My eyes snapped open. There had been a noise. I braced myself. My hand instantly slid down from my chest to my side, reaching for the homemade baton that wasn't where it should be, next to my hip. Within a second I recognized my surroundings and relaxed. No bars, no reinforced concrete ceiling hanging above me, just my childhood bedroom coming to focus in the early morning light.

I heard murmuring from outside. Two men were speaking in hushed tones as their boots crunched on the stone that covered the side yard. I couldn't make out the words but recognized Buck's distinctive voice. I rolled out from under the covers, my eye catching the bedside clock. 5:05, early even for Buck, who like me was an early riser. I awoke at approximately 5:15 every morning, laying still for five minutes before rolling out of bed to begin my calisthenics. I'd tried to sleep in after my release, but after so many years of this routine, my day didn't feel right without it. Besides, I'd earned these arms and abs and I wasn't ready to lose them.

Buck understood what life was like for me better than anyone else I knew. Long ago, the sixty-year-old had done six years of hard-time.

"Manslaughter," he'd confided in me, shortly after I'd hired him. "Killed a man in a bar fight. Didn't mean to, but I did. Donald McCallum was twenty years old -- a kid. I was younger. He had a mother and three sisters..."

"You don't have to tell me," I'd told him. I'd known Buck since I was a kid. He'd played poker with my Dad. Yet, this was the first I'd heard anything like this about the former Aussie. If my parents knew, they hadn't told me.

"I know your story, Dear," he'd replied. "It's only fair that you know mine. I wasn't a bad fella, but I wasn't that good either. Always in trouble as a kid. Petty stuff mostly. I liked breaking things: glass and fence boards, mostly. There wasn't a fence in the neighborhood that I hadn't kicked out at least one of the slats. I was marking my territory, I suppose. Anyhow, I dropped out of school and left home when I was sixteen, lied on the application and got a job on the off-shore oil rigs. I was quite a big lad and no one even questioned my age."

"I'm sure," I interjected noting our size difference. Buck was at least a head taller than me and still built quite solidly for a man in his sixties.

"When I wasn't working, I was drinking, chasing the ladies or fighting. I was good with my fists and I thought that made me a man." Buck shook his head before continuing. "One night, me and some of the boys were at a bar, just blowing off some steam after a hard week of work when this college kid, a big bloke, skipper of the university rugby team, was mouthing off to one of my friends. Needless to say, I took exception and got in his face. Soon fists were flying. He gave as good as he got. It was a good fight, I was enjoying myself, until a cue stick glanced off my head. I wrestled it from him and returned the favor. Only he went down like a sack of potatoes. I remember laughing while I poured some beer on his face to wake him up. But the poor bastard wouldn't wake up. He was in a coma for three days and then he passed."

"I'm sorry." I could see the deep regret on his face.

"Witnesses at the trial said I threw the first punch," he stated. "I probably did. I don't remember..."

"Sorry," I'd offered again, not sure what else to say.

"Don't be," Buck told me, staring into my eyes. "Things were tough inside. I took a few lickings, but it wasn't as hard for me as it was for you." He held up his hand and stopped me from speaking. "You know this is true. I eventually found my way, made some friends and learned a trade. Plus, I knew I was getting out some day. I don't know how you survived, I really don't."

"My mother," I'd replied. "I wouldn't be here, or anywhere else, without her."

"She is one hell-of-ah woman, your mother."

"The best."

"The best of the best, by a mile." Buck had agreed. "Anyway, Canada has been good for me. I've gone from breaking fences to mending them."

"How did you end up in Canada?"

"My boss, on the rigs, was Canadian," Buck laughed. "He was always bragging about his homeland. The way he described it, Canada was the greatest place on the planet. So far, I can't say that he was wrong."

"I'm surprised that you were able to emigrate with a conviction on your record," I said.

"The incident happened just before my seventeenth birthday," Buck told me. "Even though I was moved to a Federal facility when I turned eighteen, my record remained sealed. I was lucky. Here, I'm the goofy old codger who builds things. I'm literally mending fences now, but back home I'm still the bloke who killed a man."

"Thank you for sharing this with me," I'd told him, still processing the news. Buck gave off no prison vibe, never had that I could remember. Perhaps, there was hope for me. I still felt like an outsider in many situations.

103

"I know how difficult it can be adjusting to the outside. The world moves on. You discover who your true friends are and who aren't. Everyone looks at you and treats you differently." Buck said, describing my own experience to a tee. He wrapped his long arm around my shoulder. "When I got out, all I wanted was a clean, fresh start. As soon as my parole ended, I flew halfway around the world to escape my past. I ran away and that worked for me. But not you, Reggie. You face the world head on, fearlessly and with grace. Words can't express how impressed and proud I am of the way you have handled yourself, young lady."

"Thank you, Buck," I'd replied, feeling a stronger bond growing between us.

He'd given my shoulder a final squeeze and released me. "I Know that you have your mother, and some terrific young friends, but if you ever need someone to talk to, I'm available 24-7."

⤳ ⤳ ⤳

I rolled out of bed, slipped on a tee-shirt and sweat pants, swished some mouthwash, then headed down to the basement where I found Buck explaining job details, in hushed tones, to a young man about half his size.

"Reggie, I'm sorry if we woke you," Buck said, as I stepped towards them. "I called last night hoping to warn you about our early arrival."

"No worries mate." I smiled, using one of his favorite sayings on him.

"This is Darryl," Buck introduced the other man. "Darryl, this is Reggie."

"Nice to meet you Darryl," I said. Darryl's thin lips almost formed a slight smile as he nodded. His eyes were cast downward, never making contact with mine. His handshake was both firm and brief. The man was thin as a rail, but had a wiry strong look about him despite his diminutive stature. I probably had two to three inches on him. I call myself five-six, but I'm actually closer to five-foot five-and-a-half.

"Na na nice t-t-t-to me me meet-t-t-t you," he replied.

"Darryl stutters," Buck stated the obvious. "He doesn't say much, but he's the best finishing guy in the valley. There was a delay on one of his other jobs, so he suddenly has tomorrow available."

Buck had always looked past people's flaws and focused more on their abilities, so his hiring a stuttering finishing carpenter didn't seem out of place at all. The hardwood installer, had done a flawless job. Buck would only allow him on his jobsites Tuesday, Wednesday and Thursday because the man would usually be hungover from the weekend on Monday and often began weekends on Friday. Those days were some other contractor's problem.

We went over a few details, confirming the style of door and window frames I wanted. Buck suggested that we put raw cedar shelving and finishing boards in the closets to keep moths and other insects away. I liked the idea. They showed me which way the doors would swing and why. It was something I had never really put much thought into, but they had it down to a science. After about half an hour Darryl appeared comfortable that he knew exactly what was expected and was confident he'd complete our job in one day. It was kind of cute, Buck would finish most of Darryl's sentences for him. The two of them had worked together so often, they communicated in a sort of shorthand, with Darryl simply pointing at things or making simple gestures that I couldn't follow but Buck seemed to understand instantly.

They left, heading to separate projects, while I looked around my new place. The flooring and kitchen cabinetry had been completed. My suite was coming together nicely. There were still rough edges that the trim would cover and wires poking out of small holes here and there, but I could tell that Buck and his crew were doing exceptional work. Erika had suggested the chocolate milkshake color for the walls. They somehow managed to look dramatic and calming at the same time. I could hardly wait to see the contrasting white doors and floor boards against them.

The only persisting problem, and there always seems to be at least one on every construction project, was in the master bathroom. The fixtures I'd picked out had been back ordered. I stepped into the bedroom to check on the progress. There was none. The same locked unfinished temporary door blocked admittance. A warning sign taped to the door read: Danger Exposed Pipes Inside. Apparently, despite all his assurances that the bathroom would be ready by the time the rest of the house was finished, Buck had been wrong. At least the half bath in the main area was finished. It wouldn't be that much of a hardship to go upstairs and shower in Mom's place, for a while.

It was still too early to make phone calls, so I went up to my old room and did my calisthenics routine and then went for a run on the KVR trail towards Naramata. Most of the time Hannah would be waiting for me and we'd run together, but not this morning. Off to my left, an eager sailor already had his colorful orange and yellow sailed Sunfish out on the lake. Despite the negligible breeze, the sleek dinghy was gliding steadily atop the shimmering water. As I settled into a steady pace, it seemed as though we were cruising along at the same speed.

I cleared my head and for a few minutes I thought only about the rhythm of my pumping legs and arms. Even running along the razor-wire topped fences in prison, I'd felt a sense of freedom. I knew it was false, but I'd embraced it, craved it, needed it. Out here, on a day like today, with the sun warming my face and the breeze at my back, words could not describe how good I felt at these moments. I waved goodbye to the dinghy and widened my stride. I ran faster and faster until after almost a kilometer I was running flat out like a little child. Only when my heaving lungs threatened to go on strike, did I slow to a jog.

I'd come all the way to where the trail crosses Naramata Road. I had the sudden and whimsical urge to cross and just keep running. The trail goes all the way to Kelowna and beyond,

I'd been told. On my bike, I'd gone several kilometers past the village of Naramata. As tempting as the idea was, I had arrangements to make if I wanted to set up the trap for Faux J. Mavis was counting on me, too, I reminded myself. I stared up the trail for a few more seconds vowing to run, ride or hike the entire thing one day. I turned around and ran towards home.

Early the next morning, Darryl was already unloading equipment from his truck as Hannah pulled into Mom's driveway to pick me up. The three of us exchanged pleasantries, though Darryl mostly nodded and smiled nervously. The youngest of five siblings, his oldest sister had gone to school with Hannah. After Hannah managed to coax Marie's present whereabouts out of Darryl, we headed over to pick up Alan. There were few other cars on the mostly sleeping city's streets as we made two more stops before hitting the highway.

Using MapQuest, I'd determined the trip between Penticton and Canmore should take seven hours and twelve minutes. However, as we drove past a sign announcing that Canmore was just ten kilometers further I glanced at my watch. We'd barely been on the road for five hours. It didn't hurt that we were in a police cruiser and had been waved through two speed traps along the way.

I'd had plenty of time to go over the plan with Alan and the real Jennifer Gleason, while Hannah drove. Jennifer was along to make a positive ID, since the rest of us had only seen pictures of our identity thief.

Despite the short notice, Mary Beth (Faux J) had agreed to meet with Tom (Alan) for lunch at a downtown sandwich shop called 'The Range'.

Our first point of business, when we got to town, was at the local RCMP station. Hannah went in alone to inform them of our intentions. Hannah emerged from the boxy single-story building with a smile on her face and flashed us a thumbs up. They'd agreed to provide assistance. A pair of uniformed officers came out a few minutes later and jumped into an unmarked blue Charger. They followed us for a block before turning and obviously taking an alternate route.

"Is that a new shirt?" I asked Alan. I had to admit he looked good in it. The color matched his pale blue eyes perfectly.

"Yeah, I bought it yesterday," he said. "Do you like it?"

"I do," I admitted, before teasing him. "You understand that this isn't a real date, right?"

"It could be," he teased. "If she turns out not to be the identity thief, who knows what could happen?"

"Knucklehead," I said, punching his shoulder.

"I might take her back to my ranch, where we could ride horseback off into the sunset." Alan laughed, then trapped me into his long arms and began to tickle my ribs.

"Stop it," I said, trying unsuccessfully not to giggle. "I mean it."

"Only if you kiss me."

I didn't have time to agree or disagree to his terms of surrender, because his lips found mine immediately. Always just the right mix of firm and soft, I had little choice but to kiss him back.

"All right you two, break it up back there," Hannah's cop voice commanded. "We're almost there."

"Sorry Officer," Alan said, just before sneaking in another quick kiss. "It won't happen again."

"That's better, now keep those hands where I can see them, Mister," she chuckled, winking at us through the rear view mirror as she drove along a deserted tree-lined street.

I glanced over at Jennifer. She forced a smile, but I could tell she was nervous about the upcoming encounter with Faux J. I couldn't blame her. The woman had been her best friend before stealing her identity and ruining her life. I indicated to Alan to settle down.

"This will be over before you know it, Jennifer," I assured her. She nodded and forced another smile. I put on my game face and began to mentally prepare myself.

"How's my hair?" Alan asked. There was still some impishness in his voice.

I shook my head, fished a mirror out of my purse and held it up for him.

Alan made a few adjustments with his fingertips, then looked deeply into his own eyes. "Hi Mary Beth, I'm Tom." He pantomimed shaking hands, then cracked a big smile. "Do you want to get out of here and go horseback riding?"

"Toss me your gun," I said to Hannah.

"We need him alive for now," Hannah retorted, then raised her baton. "Will this do?"

"Perfect."

"Okay, okay," Alan said. "I'll be serious. I'm ready." He leaned back into his seat and mumbled quietly, "Some people have no sense of humor."

Alan looked so cute when he pouted. Under different circumstances I'd have undone my seatbelt and been all over him. Realizing Hannah was watching me and had read my mind, I blushed. She smiled.

We had no trouble finding the restaurant since it was located right on Main Street. We'd arrived a half hour early. Hannah dropped us off at the corner and then drove off to stash the car out of sight. I entered first, to make certain Faux J wasn't already inside. The inside reminded me of a ranch house. The roasting meats from the nearby ovens smelled great. Mary Beth wasn't amongst the early lunch crowd. I signaled for Alan and Jennifer to enter.

We positioned Alan in a booth by the side windows and seated him facing the front door so Mary Beth could easily see him when she entered. Jennifer and I took the last table near the rear exit with her back to the entrance. Hannah was to rendezvous with her RCMP counterparts across the street in the London Drugs.

To authenticate our covers Jennifer and I ordered food. I opted for the daily special – Roasted Alberta Beef with balsamic onions, arugula, mustard and parmesan aioli. It sounded great. Jennifer ordered a quinoa salad. Even salads had changed while I'd been in prison. Since my release, I'd heard of this new supposedly healthy ancient-grain but had never tried it. Sounded like a 'fad' food to me. I still subscribed to the tried and true 'eat vegetables and fruit every day' plan.

Alan sat alone with only a glass of water, waiting for his 'date' to arrive.

The popular lunch spot was filling up. I'd barely eaten a third of my amazing sandwich when a young woman stepped through the door. Her distinctive eyes swept the restaurant. I tilted my gaze slightly away to avoid eye contact. Faux J's face lit up with a big smile when Alan stood and waved at her. She started toward him.

"Hey!" A woman sitting at the table next to Jennifer and I, said rather loudly. "You're the cop that was in prison, aren't you?"

I tried to appease her with a polite, please don't bother me right now, half-smile. She was oblivious.

"It is you, the one they called Black Swan. I recognize you from the news," she exclaimed, as she stood and dug a phone from her pocket. "You helped catch that serial killer over in Penticton, right?"

By now everyone in the restaurant was staring at me, including Faux J, who was in the middle of shaking hands with Alan. Our eyes locked for a couple of seconds. We'd never met before, but I could see the mention of Penticton had put her on alert. Real Jennifer turned to look at her. Faux J's eyes widened in recognition of her former victim.

"That's her," real Jennifer confirmed.

"What's going on here, Tom?" Faux J yanked her hand from Alan's, then turned and started toward the front of the restaurant. She stopped in her tracks. Hannah and the two highly-visible Mounties were halfway across the street, marching rapidly our way.

"Can I get a selfie?" the annoying woman asked.

"Maybe later," I said, standing to block the rear exit. I had a feeling Faux J would try to make a run for it. I stepped between real Jennifer and the fake, bracing myself for the charge. We'd planned to send Jennifer over to make the identification once

Hannah and her new RCMP buddies were in the restaurant. Things seldom go exactly as planned, but at least the filly had been corralled; now we needed to separate her from the herd and put a halter on her. This country jargon could be addictive.

Faux J's face contorted. Trapped animals are the most dangerous. I had pepper spray in my purse, but there wouldn't be time to grab it. She glanced at the door and then at me. At five foot five and a half, I'm not exactly an imposing figure. She barreled at me.

"Stop!" I shouted, holding my hand outward like I was halting traffic. She didn't stop. I wasn't surprised. My hand wasn't out there simply for show, though. I caught her shoulder with a Walter Payton style stiff arm. My Dad and I used to watch NFL games together every Sunday. I was such a tomboy. 'Da Bears' were my favorite. Faux J twisted and deflected to my left. With my knees already bent and tilted slightly outward, I simply pushed my left one further left catching her leading leg. Faux J's feet tangled and she spun hard, tumbling out of control past me, colliding with my vacated chair. Her flailing hand grasped desperately, sweeping the contents from the top of our table. Faux J ended up in a heap on the floor, covered in quinoa and balsamic onions.

I pulled plasti-cuffs from my pocket and zipped them around the stunned woman's wrists. I might have put them on a little tighter than necessary. But in all fairness, she had destroyed my sandwich.

"That was amazing," Annoying Woman called out. Then from behind her a more familiar voice spoke out.

"Looks like we missed all the fun," Hannah said, as I yanked Faux J to her feet and passed her to one of the Mounties.

"Oh my God," Annoying Woman exclaimed to everyone in the restaurant. "It's Hannah Buckley, the cop that caught the TransCanada Killer."

An excited crowd instantly began to gather around Hannah.

"You single-handedly saved that woman that everyone thought was dead," a man said.

"Would you sign my book?" Another man asked. "I have a copy in my car. I'll run out and get it."

I lowered my head and crept away, leaving Hannah to deal with the adoring fans.

Outside, Jennifer confronted Faux J. One RCMP officer held her at arm's length, trying unsuccessfully to avoid getting quinoa on his clean uniform, while the other went to get the car.

"We were friends. How could you do this to me? You hurt a lot of people."

Faux J didn't acknowledge Jennifer or her questions. She refused to even look at the woman whose life she'd stolen and ruined. There was no remorse on that glassy-eyed, mayo-stained, but otherwise blank face. I'd dealt with many psychopaths in my time. Hell, I'd lived with dozens of them while in prison. They were bereft of empathy. I'd learned that every smile which crossed their face or nice thing they'd ever done for anyone else was calculated to benefit themselves in some way.

"Why?" Jennifer demanded, as the Charger pulled up.

I walked over and put my arm around Jennifer's shoulder. "You won't get any answers from her. She was never really your friend. She's incapable of real feelings for anybody but herself."

"At least you helped put away a very bad person today," Alan added, joining us. We watched as Faux J was stuffed into the back of the Mountie's police car.

Fifteen minutes and many, many autographs later, Hannah came out of 'The Range' carrying a large bag.

"Sandwiches for the trip home," she informed us. I crossed my fingers hoping there was at least one Roasted Alberta Beef inside.

We followed the cruiser back to the RCMP station. Hannah spoke to the officer in charge for several minutes, while Faux J was finger printed and photographed. I couldn't help but notice how neat and organized the place was. There wasn't a sheet of paper or pen out of place. I dragged my finger across the top of a file cabinet. It came up dust-free.

"Her real name is Roxanne Morton and she faces dozens of charges of identity theft and fraud from all across Western Canada," Hannah told us.

Roxanne? I'd never have guessed her real name. She didn't look like a Roxanne to me. Though what did I know? I glanced up at the photo of our young Prime Minister hanging next to the Queen. To me he looked more like a pharmacist than the leader of a nation.

"The Winnipeg RCMP Anti-Fraud office has a fairly extensive file on Miss Morton. Apparently, she stole her mother's credit card when she was seventeen, ran away from home and has been stealing identities ever since," Hannah continued. "According to the file, they had been close to catching Morton a couple times, but through good fortune or cunning she has always stayed a step ahead."

"Probably a little bit of both," I commented, begrudgingly admitting that the woman had been very good at her ill-chosen profession.

"The team in Winnipeg are very impressed with your little sting operation," Hannah said, slapping me on the back. "They send their congratulations."

"What will happen to Faux-J now?" Alan asked Hannah, still using the name we'd given Morton.

"She'll be held here until it is determined where and when she'll face charges and I'm certain some very serious jail time."

Real Jennifer suddenly threw her arms around me and sobbed 'thank you' over and over quietly into my ear. I hugged back tightly feeling her relief that this whole affair was finally over, and I had to acknowledge a profound satisfaction of my own. When her sobbing subsided, I might also have sobbed a couple times, she released me and turned to Alan and Hannah, "Thank you all. You guys are amazing."

The ride home was filled with laughter and jubilation.

CHAPTER 13

I awoke as the first rays of the sun filtered through the curtains. I felt pretty good considering the amount of sleep I'd gotten the night before. Yesterday had been successful, but long. After providing statements and filling with gas, it had been after four pm by the time we'd hit the road home.

Still sound asleep, Alan stirred and rolled over onto his stomach as I slipped out from under the sheets. He'd wasted no time at all collecting on the promises I'd made for his help in our little caper, insisting I stay over. Looking at those shoulders and his wide muscular back tempted me to crawl right back in with him. He looked so peaceful, I resisted the urge.

It took some doing but I finally located my bra (which I found in the hallway) along with both my socks. I raided Alan's closet and donned a pair of his running shorts, which fit better than I wanted to admit to myself and a t-shirt that I had to tie a knot around the waist of to stop from slipping off my shoulders. I crept downstairs to the living room and began my morning calisthenics routine. This was my equivalent to a morning cup of coffee. Unless I'd been in the infirmary, this was how I'd started each day in prison as I waited for my cell door to open. Out for well over a year now, my day still didn't feel right without starting this way. Plus, it kept me in shape. I preferred my pushups, leg raises, lunges, wall sits, chair dips and fingertip pullups to pumping iron at the gym. Alan understood. Occasionally, I'd do my routine at his fitness center, but I could do it anywhere. After an hour I felt energized and ready to take on the world.

Alan's little two-story house was in a near-perfect location. Just a block and a half from the main beach, you could walk to every restaurant and venue in downtown Penticton. This morning I headed in the opposite direction toward the channel that travels approximately five point five kilometers from Lake Okanagan down to Skaha Lake. During hot summer days, the waterway was filled with tire tubes and air mattresses of all shapes and sizes. I'd tubed the channel many times myself when I was younger.

I would run from lake to lake and back every time I stayed over at Alan's. He tried to run with me one morning, but my pace was pretty fast and he ended up walking most of the way back. He pretended it was okay, but I think it bruised his male ego just a little. Occasionally, I'd meet up with Hannah and we'd run it together, but not this morning. I was on my own. I didn't mind at all. Running for me is like meditation. I think while I run. Now that Faux J had been captured I could concentrate fully on solving Milo's murder.

I crossed the channel bridge, where Highway Ninety-Seven bends to join up with Eckhart, and went down the bank to the trail. I'd retied the knot to get it out of the way and stuffed it into Alan's shorts at the back. It probably looked like I had the world's worst case of hemorrhoids, but I didn't want all that extra material flapping around while I ran. The water in the channel flowed lazily towards Skaha Lake. There was hardly a cloud in the brightening sky and almost no breeze to speak of. It looked to be another hot sunny day in the Okanagan, but at this hour there was still a chill in the air. I rubbed the goosebumps from my forearms, stretched out my calves and quads and then started. Once I'd gone a kilometer or two, I'd generate enough of my own heat to keep me warm.

I exchanged "Good Mornings," when a pair of seniors passed me on bikes. They appeared to be well into their seventies and still going strong. Maybe that would be Alan and me someday. The thought brought a smile to my face. My stride got a little bouncier.

I'd just made the turn-around at Skaha Lake and was heading back when I first felt it. As a cop, I'd learned to listen to my gut, but as an inmate I'd trusted it with my life. I was the target of someone's interest, I could feel it. My senses went into overdrive. I made a conscious effort to hide my awareness. My stride went unchanged and I fought the urge to look over my shoulder. I scanned the trail ahead carefully. Aside from a woman, whom I'd seen other similar mornings, playing fetch with her golden retriever I could see nothing out of the ordinary. I listened past the steady pat, pat, pat of my feet striking the dirt path for other footfalls on or off the path around me. I heard none.

I veered off the path, to a nearby bench and pretended to tie my shoe. I stole a glance at the trail behind. It was empty.

"You're just paranoid, Reggie," I whispered to myself, unconvincingly.

The toaster popped as I walked in the back door. I'd done my cool down walk along the lakeshore and gotten home exactly one hour from the time I'd left.

"I'm that predictable?" I asked, already knowing the answer. Even without trying, my run and cool off walk always took exactly an hour. Coincidentally, it was the amount of time I'd been allowed in the 'yard' during my eight-year vacation in federal custody.

"I heard you head out at six fifteen." We both glanced up at the kitchen clock. Seven fifteen, exactly. "Plus, I spotted you coming up the alley, so I threw the toast in."

Alan slid a spinach and cheese egg-white omelet onto a slice of whole wheat toast and set it on the counter in front of me. There were already two sitting in the plate next to mine. Alan brought two tumblers of ice-water with him as he sat beside me. He leaned over and kissed the back of my still-damp neck. There was no point in protesting, his work shirt stated right across the front 'I like sweat!' I was reminded of the first time I saw the new improved Alan and his shirt. We'd bumped into each other at the yogurt aisle in Safeway more than a year ago. Time flies by when you have a wonderful boyfriend.

"Uhm, salty and sweet," he said, as my hackles finally began to relax.

"I guess that makes me the kettle corn of girlfriends," I responded, just before downing half the water in my glass. I decided not to say anything about feeling watched to him. I didn't want him to worry. Besides, it might just have been a bout of paranoia, I tried again, unsuccessfully to convince myself.

"Kettle corn is my favorite." Alan smiled, then started in on his eggs.

"This is really good," I told him, after my first bite. "I should let you make breakfast for me every morning."

"I could get used to this, too." He nudged his big shoulder against mine.

I'd fallen for this guy. Alan had said the words out loud. I hadn't. For me, saying I'm in love with you was virtually the same as uttering I do at a church in front of friends and family. Being 'In love' with someone is huge -- a forever commitment. I'd made a forever commitment once before. I'd meant it when I said, 'For richer or poorer, for better or worse.' I thought Trent had, too. Granted, your wife spending the rest of her life in prison is near the far end of the 'for worse' scale, but I believe that I'd have stood by him. Part of me understood and even wanted Trent to have a life without me. It made perfect sense. He was a young man; he could start over. However, receiving the annulment papers without warning had scarred me in more ways than one. He'd acted like everything was okay when he'd visited me just two weeks earlier. I couldn't believe that the man I was 'in love' with could be so cold, calculating and cruel to me. I couldn't make sense of it at the time.

I'd been so shocked, I'd walked around like a zombie. Usually vigilant, my guard was down, and sure enough, I never saw the attack coming. Only my magazines and constant training had saved me. I'd been fortunate not to die that day; the day Trent abandoned me. Making the commitment again was going to be hard for me. I'd told Alan that much, at least. He said that he understood, and seemed to. Alan had passed every boyfriend test with flying colors, yet I kept him on permanent probation, poor guy. I was so lucky to have someone like him in my life. I nudged him back.

We ate mostly in silence. Alan had his giant phone next to his plate. He was on Kijiji looking at scooters. I'd told him how much I loved riding Betsy and let him take her out for a spin. He'd returned after about twenty minutes with a huge grin plastered across his face. He'd been talking about getting his own ever since.

"This Zhang Xing 150 looks pretty sporty," he said, holding up his phone for me to see.

The red and black bike looked more like a sport racer than a scooter. "I don't know anything about Chinese bikes, but I think you'd be better off with a Honda or Vespa and a few more cc's if you ever want to take it on the highway."

"Yeah, you're right," he said. "I just thought it looked pretty sharp, is all."

Alan insisted upon cleaning up the dishes, while I took a shower. I put on yesterday's slacks, a different but still oversized t-shirt and headed down stairs. He'd already left for work, but there was a note left on the counter.

Sweetheart,
It was great working with you yesterday and
even better ending and starting my day with you.
When you're ready, I will make you breakfast
every morning for the rest of your life.

I Love you, Alan
Ps. Did I mention that I'm in love with you?

Wow. My knees went weak. I lifted the note to my heart.

"I'm in love with you, too," I said out loud for the first time, to the empty house. It was a start. Baby steps.

I locked up and headed home to change into my work clothes. I had people to see and a murder case to solve.

CHAPTER 14

Buck was in the driveway when I pulled up. I knew that he noticed my still-damp hair, but he didn't say anything about it. He had a serious look on his face. The city inspector had been to the house yesterday and I didn't need any more bad news.

"She's right up to code," he reported, finally breaking into a smile.

"Wow, that's great news," I said, rushing over to give him a big bear hug. I couldn't believe it. We'd had to put in a larger electrical panel and rewire the whole basement to accommodate the new kitchen and bathroom. That, plus all the additional plumbing, had to pass the city inspections.

"We should be able to clean up all the little odds and ends by the end of the day," Buck told me. "I'll come over tomorrow morning and we can do a final walkthrough together. If that works for you?"

"That would be fantastic!"

Part of me wanted to rush right down and have a look, but I decided to wait until the next morning. My very own place. I'd never actually lived alone before. I'd lived in the dorms during university and while at the Police Academy, then shared an apartment with Rose Fennel, a beautician, until I moved in with and later married Trent. I'd had my own cell in prison, but it certainly wasn't private. I was excited. Mom would be just upstairs, but that didn't matter to me. In fact, that made it even better. My mom had always been a great mom, wife and homemaker. I loved her. She'd been very nurturing, though occasionally strict to the point of annoyance, she was always there for me when I needed her. I'd lived with her for eighteen-plus years, yet besides being my mom, I'd hardly known who she really was. I'd been a Daddy's girl. I'd always believed that I took after him. I'd wanted to be just like him. My father had been strong, smart and easy going.

Championing the cause to get me out of prison, my mom had shown me what real strength was. Through every setback and outright failure, she had never once wavered in her resolve to get me free. She only fought harder. Her absolute belief in my innocence was as strong as my own, somehow maybe stronger. Her positive reinforcement kept me going. During my stay in prison, I started to see her as more than just a mother. I finally saw her as the strong woman she was and, I began to realize, had always been. Seeing me close to death in the prison infirmary had broken my father. It made Mom more determined. She would not quit. My mom gave me life twice. Neither time had been easy. Having her nearby was both comforting and a privilege.

I waved as Buck pulled his big Ford F350 out of the driveway and then headed inside.

"How did things go yesterday, Sweetheart?" Mom asked. She was standing with her back to me, cleaning up her breakfast dishes. Mom always seemed to get both the first and the last words in our conversations. She knew about the little sting operation we'd planned.

"Very well," I said, walking over and giving her a hug from behind. "Alan did a great job and I got to tackle her."

"Good for you," Mom said. I still hadn't let go of her.

"My clients are very happy, I'm happy, Hannah's happy," I told her, squeezing tighter. "That woman won't be ruining anyone else's life for a very long time. So, it was a very good day. Thank you, Mom."

"Why are you thanking me?" Mom asked, without turning around. "You caught her."

"I never thought I'd have days like that ever again. Thank you, thank you, thank you. You're my hero. You gave my life back to me," I told her, amid another hug. "If it wasn't for you, I'd still be rotting in prison."

"The truth would have come out eventually, Reggie, with or without my help," Mom said, trying to deflect the credit.

"I don't think so." We'd gotten into this debate several times before. It usually led to a discussion about who really saved Amy Connelly.

"Besides, the real murderer is in prison now because of you. You're the one who saved Amy's life -- you're the real hero."

Mom had been right beside me when I'd come up with the serial killer theory. For reasons she could never quite manage to accept, I'd decided to give most of the credit for that and a few other things to Hannah. I was perfectly happy with how things turned out. For one thing, it saved Hannah's job and in our version of events I didn't look like the schmuck that was dating a serial killer. I'd been a covert operative gathering intel on our prime suspect until things went wrong and he took me hostage. Then, along came Hannah to save the day. That part was true. We'd also left out the part where I was on the verge of escaping to get help when she arrived. However, I got my small, but heroic moment in the newspapers and book, when I distracted the TransCanada Killer long enough for Hannah to wound him with her last and final bullet. After Hannah winged him, I'd tackled and pinned the bastard down while Hannah threw on the plasti-cuffs. Though that part of his capture had come off a little anti-climactic in the book version, Mom had often complained. I didn't care.

"We're both heroes," I compromised, giving Mom a final squeeze and a kiss on the back of her neck.

"I just wish..."

"Hannah is pregnant," I blurted out news that I knew would halt our current discussion, though I instantly regretted it. I'd have to tell Hannah.

"That's wonderful news," Mom said, finally turning around to face me.

"She and Danny are very excited," I told her.

"I bet they are."

"This is just between us," I warned Mom. "She hasn't told anyone at work about it yet, so you can't tell your friends."

"The Buckleys are having a baby," Mom said, ignoring my warning.

"I'm serious Mom, you can't tell anyone yet."

"I heard you the first time," Mom conceded.

"Good, because this kind of news travels fast."

"Can I get you something to eat, Sweetheart?"

"Thanks, but Alan made me breakfast before he went to work," I informed her. "I just need to change my clothes so I can get to work myself."

"I noticed that Buck was here. Did you get a chance to talk to him before he left?"

"Yes," I said, happy to be onto a different subject. "The place passed inspection. We're doing the final walkthrough tomorrow."

"That's great," Mom said.

"You're welcome to join us," I said. "In fact, you should. You might spot something that I miss."

"Thank you, I'd love that." Mom turned and grabbed a notepad from the window sill above the sink. "I've made a list of furniture, linens and dishes that you can have for your new place."

"Oh Mom, you don't have to do that."

"I have a lot of duplicates," she said, handing the pad to me.

"Apparently," I said, flipping quickly through several pages of items. "We can go through this tonight, okay?"

"Okay," she said, then gave me a hug. "Reggie, it makes me so happy to see you enjoying life again."

"I'm happy that you're happy about my happiness," I laughed, then got serious. It was my turn to hug her. I whispered into her ear, "Thank you, Mom. Every good moment I have in my life is because you saved me."

"Reggie..."

"You know that, right?" I kissed her cheek and stepped back.

"Get out of here before you make me cry." Mom dismissed me with the wave of one hand, while the other wiped away a tear.

"I should be home by dinner," I said, kissing her one more time before heading toward my room.

"I'm having dinner with friends," Mom called to me.

"Okay, see you when you get home," I yelled, from halfway up the stairs.

I threw on grey slacks and a white blouse with grey collars and cuffs and comfortable low-heeled shoes. There would be a lot of walking and standing today. I checked to make certain I had enough business cards in my purse. There probably were, but I grabbed a couple dozen more from my desk. I tested both my pens and then tucked them and a fresh notepad into my purse as well. I moved the small unmarked bottle of pepper-spray, which had worked its way down to the bottom of my purse, back up to the top.

After my encounter with the TransCanada Killer, where I'd been caught without a weapon, I loaded up my purse. Inside was a small multitool device with pliers, screw drivers and a razor-sharp blade. Hidden in the tear-away side lining, a folding knife with a four-inch-long blade and a slender but comfortable rubber grip. For eighty-five bucks, I'd purchased a very good quality collapsible aluminum baton. In police academy, we'd been taught baton basics as part of our weapon training. In prison, thousands of hours of practice alone in my cell had made me quite proficient with the weapon. A tightly rolled magazine had saved my bacon on several occasions. I removed the baton from my handbag and slipped it into my pants pocket. I guess this morning's run had spooked me more than I realized, because I did something I hadn't done for many months. I rolled up my sleeves and strapped a magazine to each of my forearms, just as I had every time I left my cell.

I rebuttoned my cuffs and checked to see that the magazines weren't visible. They felt good, perhaps too good, like I'd just been wrapped in a security blanket. I reminded myself that normal people don't cover themselves with magazines and that this was a temporary measure.

I added the party guest list to my purse and headed out to find the person who'd killed Milo Getz.

CHAPTER 15

As I rolled Betsy out of the garage, the feeling of being watched returned. This time even stronger. Without being overt, I surveyed my surroundings. The neighborhood looked normal, although there was a dark sedan parked at the corner two blocks down, that I didn't recognize.

Halfway down the street, Mrs. Underwood and her latest Pekinese pal were out for their morning walk. She'd gotten her first Pekinese puppy the day after her husband's passing. He, apparently, wouldn't have a pet in their house. The Widow Underwood had already been an old lady back when I was kid playing in the neighborhood. She'd always had a stick of gum or a mint candy for me when I'd stop and pet her dog. She must be ninety-five or ninety-six by now, I realized. I waved to her and she waved back, then turned into her yard, four houses down from ours. Mrs. Underwood, even Mom referred to her formally, still maintained her property including a good-sized garden by herself. Mom often said that she wanted to be like Mrs. Underwood when she grows up. We should all aspire to that. I decided that I would make the time to stop in for a visit in the next day or two.

I turned my attention back to the sedan: two-door model, navy, probably a Nissan or Mazda. I couldn't make out the plate from this distance. I pulled out of the driveway and headed the opposite direction. When I reached Vancouver Avenue, I checked my mirror. The sedan hadn't moved. I pulled onto Vancouver and headed up toward Naramata Road.

After speaking with the Martins, Rosemary Eberle and her husband Damien had risen to the top of my list. Fallen Leaves Wines turned out to be a modest operation compared to Butterface, but there was an old European charm to the property and buildings. The grounds were spotless and well kept. The tasting room was attached to the east side of the 'gingerbread' style house. Tastings started at 11:00 am according to a small sign in the window.

From the corner of my eye, as I removed my helmet, I spotted a navy vehicle go past on the road. I turned my head, but it was gone from sight. I hadn't gotten a good enough look to determine whether or not it was the same car.

As I swung my leg off Betsy, a short roundish man emerged from the closest door. If he'd been wearing a floppy hat, he could have easily passed for a Keebler elf.

"Good morning, young lady," he said in deep, very non-Keebler elf, voice. His wide genuine smile lit up the weathered but pleasant face. The deep creases in his face suggested that he smiled a lot. There was an air of contentment surrounding him. I had a great first impression of the man.

"Good morning, to you sir," I replied, as I stored my helmet. "Mr. Eberle?"

"Please, call me Damien," he said, stepping out onto the stone patio between us. His eyes sparkled, below a thick mane of grey and black speckled hair. I shook his firm, muscular hand.

"Thank you, Damien, I'm Reggie, Reggie Swann."

"Lizzie's daughter?" he asked and I nodded in response. "I heard you had returned to town. Welcome home."

"Thank you, it's nice to be back."

"You're not here for a sample, I take it," he stated, still smiling.

"No," I admitted. "I'm investigating the death of your neighbor. I was hoping to speak to both you and your wife about Milo and the night he died."

"I see," he replied, then tilted his head toward the house. "Let's go inside."

I don't know what I expected to find, but it wasn't the thoroughly modern, stainless steel and granite kitchen that we walked into. The savory smells wafting from the large double ovens were heavenly. Flour and small pieces of dough on the nearby counter suggested pastries.

Rosemary Eberle was several centimeters taller than her husband and rail thin. Bulging eyes, a long protruding nose and thin lips gave her a hawk-like appearance. She wasn't smiling.

"Hello," I offered.

She stared at me blankly for a few seconds, then turned a harsh eye to her husband.

"Whatever she's selling I'm not interested," Rosemary snapped. There was just the hint of an Eastern European influence in the cadence of her words. She raised her flour-caked hands. "Can't you see that I'm busy?"

"She's not a salesman, Rosie," Damien quickly asserted. "She's Lizzy Swann's daughter."

"So?" Her eyes returned to mine without softening.

"Hello," I said again, widening my smile, but to no avail. Her expression didn't waiver. "I'm investigating the death of Milo Getz."

"What's to investigate? He drowned in a vat of wine, didn't he?"

"Yes," I conceded, and then countered with, "but there was a possibility of foul play."

"Not according to the papers, there wasn't."

"Mrs. Getz, Mavis, hired me to look into her husband's demise," I said. Immediately, the demeanor of the woman in front of me relaxed.

"That poor woman." Rosemary's voice was softer, her face awash with sympathy. The change was remarkable. "What can we do to help?"

"Can you tell me about the night of the party?"

"It was quite the event," Damien happily piped in. "Everyone was there."

"I only went because of Mavis," Rosemary pointed out. "She's a peach, that woman. But him…"

"Rosemary, give it a rest," Damien cut her off. "The man is dead."

"I don't care," Rosemary spat out. I could see this was a sore spot between the two of them. "I didn't like him, his music or the names of his wine. Who calls a table wine Zipper Ripper Red?"

"That was a marketing strategy and it worked," Damien pointed out. "Zipper Ripper and Bleached Blonde are two of the best-selling Canadian wines in North America."

"Maybe so," she said. "I find the names quite disrespectful."

"What time did you arrive at the party?" I asked, filling the short silence that followed.

"We got there about seven-thirty," Damien answered.

"That's right," Rosemary confirmed. "Then I spent the next two hours avoiding Ivy Martin."

"Rosemary." Damien shook his head. "This feud between the two of you has to stop."

"Every time I run into that woman she brags about how many bottles they've sold or what their tasting receipts are for the week."

"I'm happy for all their success," Damien said.

"Humph." Rosemary rolled her eyes before turning to check on whatever she had baking in the oven.

"Before Butterface moved in between us, Fallen Leaves and Crooked Tree were about the same size. We had a friendly rivalry. Every Monday, the four of us would go out for dinner and compare notes. We worked together, often combining promotions for the benefit of each other," Damien explained.

"Now their sales have doubled and ours have only seen, well, modest improvements."

"Why is that?" I asked.

"It isn't because their wine is better than ours, I'll tell you that much," Rosemary said, as she removed a large pan of golden brown pastries.

"Most of the wine tours start at the Penticton end of the benches and work their way north toward the village of Naramata. It has always been a challenge for the wineries furthest north to attract big numbers of tourists," Damien explained.

"It is my understanding that Milo had been good for Okanagan wine sales," I said.

"Since the arrival of Butterface, interest in the Okanagan wineries has increased tenfold. Everyone here has benefited to some degree. Our wines are in stores all across the country. However, like most small operations, onsite sales are a vital part of our business. Those wineries south of Butterface..."

"Like the Martins," Rosemary interjected.

"...have benefited greatly from increased walk in traffic, while those of us to the north haven't benefitted quite as much."

"Why is that?" I wondered aloud.

"For obvious reasons Butterface Wines has become the main attraction for those coming to the region. It has a big, beautiful tasting room. There is always great music and food, plus, you might get to take a selfie with the legend himself."

"Not anymore," Rosemary added, morbidly.

"No, I guess not," Damien conceded, before continuing. "Professional tours and people out tasting on their own, tend to make Butterface their final stop. The tasting part of our business, and that of the other four wineries north of Butterface, consists mostly of the more serious wine..." he hesitated for a second before continuing, "... I was going to say connoisseurs, but that isn't the right word, let's call them wine buffs, who come back the next day and continue to the tour the bench. But they are just a small percentage."

"I understand you had an altercation with Milo at the party," I said directly to Rosemary.

"What!" Damien exclaimed. "I didn't know anything about this."

"Not an altercation, really," Rosemary said. "I just offered a few suggestions to him that evening."

"What did you do?" Damien asked, accusingly.

"I just felt that he and his staff should direct more customers our way. Maybe display some of our new banners in his parking lot."

"Rosemary," he said, his voice heavy with disappointment. "You saw with your own eyes that he'd put up the 'Tour Naramata North's Wineries' poster right next to the exit door in the tasting room. He didn't have to do that."

"I know that," Rosemary murmured. "I guess I got a little jealous when I saw how many people were there."

"Rosie," he said, this time sympathetically. Damien walked over and put his arm around his wife's shoulders. "We had our twenty-fifth anniversary five weeks ago and only about forty people came by."

"It's my fault," Rosemary said, her voice cracking with regret. "I've become a miserable old woman. I say things that I regret. I've pushed away most of our friends. If not for you, we'd have none."

"Not true, Rosie," Damien said, stroking her face.

"I'm sorry," Rosemary said to me, wiping away a tear that escaped. "What you must think of me…"

"We've all said or done things we regret," I told her truthfully. Recently, I'd come to the realization that during the last few years in prison, I had begun to welcome confrontations. I didn't look for trouble, but I didn't avoid it either. It had become a deadly game to me, but the stakes hadn't really seemed that high to me then. Despite my mother's undying optimism, a part of me had come to believe my only way out of prison was inside a pine box. Leaving in the box, sooner rather than later, didn't have much meaning to me then. I didn't want to die, but I'd gotten to the point that I no longer feared that outcome. I knew in my bones that eventually my time would come. In that place, the chances were zero out of a hundred that I would pass away peacefully of old age.

At some point, I'm not certain exactly when, I'd begun to take a perverse pleasure in seeing the scars, bruises and bandages on the faces and bodies of those who'd come at me. I was no longer simply fighting off the aggressors, I'd begun purposely marking them. At the time, I convinced myself those scars were walking billboards, warning others to leave me alone. In truth, they were more. I hate that I'd let myself drop to that level. I'd gone from protecting and serving, to maiming and harming. Life had become a lot less precious to me, though I'm certain that I'd never have fallen far enough to intentionally take one. Well, I'm almost certain that day would never have come, and that slight doubt was a regret I'd have to carry with me forever.

"Believe me," I added.

Rosemary kissed her husband's cheek and took a few seconds to compose herself. "What would you like to know?"

CHAPTER 16

As soon as I'd stepped out of the Eberle's house, I felt eyes on me again. I'll admit to being overly sensitive, but in prison when I was the focus of someone's attention it had never once been a good thing. Over time, I became quite attuned to these feelings. Even though I could not see whoever it was, I knew they were out there watching me. I didn't know why, but my alarm bells were ringing. As I slid onto Betsy, my fingers grazed the baton in my pocket, providing a small measure of comfort to my growing anxiety. *Who could be watching me?*

"I love my life," I whispered, as the realization hit me like a ton of bricks. I have purpose beyond simple survival. There are people I care about and that care about me. I'm genuinely happy for the first time in a long time. The last time I'd felt like this I was a homicide detective, married to the man of my dreams and Dad was still alive. I'd lost the things dearest to me, and for a very long time life had little value or meaning to me.

Freedom, friends and a future – three things I'd learned the true value of once I'd regained them. The faces of the most important people in my life flashed through my mind – Mom, Alan, Hannah, Danny, Erika, Rhonda, Robert... I love these guys.

I'm in love with one of them. I have a life worth fighting for and I would. I scanned the area as I approached Naramata Road, but could see no sign of the source of my nervousness. I twisted the throttle and headed further north.

I hadn't learned much new information from the Eberles. Though, Damien mentioned seeing a man that night who seemed out of place and had been staring at Milo with an odd expression on his face. Damien had never seen him before, so the fellow wasn't local or a regional winemaker. He'd tried to strike up a conversation with the guy, but the man excused himself and walked away without offering his name. That had been at approximately 8 pm, inside the tasting room. I made a note to check the security tapes.

As I was about to turn into the driveway of the next winery on my list, I spotted a dark blue car in my rearview mirror. I stopped and twisted around on my seat so I could get a good look at the driver. It was a woman with two small kids in the back seat of a station wagon. I made note of her face, though I was pretty sure she wasn't my watcher. I doubted that someone would have rented children to provide cover. Where would you even do that? I chased the both silly and repulsive idea from my head. Plus, the car I'd seen near Mom's place had been a sedan. Disappointed, I continued into the Spotted Fawn Winery.

I'd spent the rest of the morning and most of the afternoon interviewing growers and winemakers up and down the eastern benches between Penticton and Naramata. All had confirmed benefitting from the increased interest and activity Butterface Wine and Milo himself had generated for the area. I'd noted varying degrees of awe, jealousy and respect towards Milo from most of the owners, but so far I hadn't come across anyone who seemed like a viable suspect. I was beginning to think I was barking up the wrong tree. Maybe the killer was a crazed music fan or just another Mark David Chapman type. It was easy to get distracted during an investigation. Sometimes you had to put in the hard yards. Most leads didn't pan out, but if you didn't pull at every thread you might miss something important. The most successful investigators I'd worked with during my career as a police detective were both methodical and open minded. My last partner used to say if you open enough doors the bad guy will be behind one of them.

Eight vineyard owners from the other side of the lake had attended the Butterface anniversary party. By five-thirty I'd talked with half of them. Over on the west benches, Milo's impact hadn't been felt nearly as much as east of the lake. The wine tours on the east side were more established and it didn't hurt that the KVR trail was better developed through that area. Since most of the wineries were easily accessible from both Naramata Road, which wound charmingly through the eastern benches, and the KVR trail, tourists had many wine tasting options including walking, biking, self-driving and fully-guided bus tours.

Though they were scattered, seemingly haphazardly, I'd been surprised at the number of wineries in the rolling hills around Summerland. So far, I'd found the winery owners here to be fiercely proud of both their wine and the steadily growing interest in wine production in the Summerland region. There was respect, though sometimes grudging, for what Milo had accomplished personally and for the Naramata wine growers in general. I hadn't gotten the impression that anyone I'd spoken to, so far, had motive to wish Milo harm.

Next on the list was Ross Gregory, owner of Gregory Estates Winery. I'd been waiting to talk to Mr. Gregory. He was the man who'd sold his former winery to Milo Getz and one of the last people to see Milo alive. I pulled out my notes and flipped to my interview with the Martins. According to them, Gregory had been part of the anti-Milo coalition, and on top of that he'd been quite upset when he found out that his prized vines had been dug up and replaced. I was reminded of that story when I came across Malbec scribbled in the margin.

I pulled back onto the street and headed west on Prairie Valley Rd. Gregory Estates Winery was only a kilometer further. On top of the being-stalked sensation that had doggedly followed me all day, I felt another familiar twinge start to build in my bones. One I used to feel before I'd begin an interrogation or confront a subject of interest. If unchecked, it would grow until I felt like I could shoot electricity from my fingertips. Unfortunately, that had never actually happened. That would have been cool. I willed myself to stay calm. I chalked it up to badly needing a suspect in this case.

When I first drove through the gates, I was hit with a sense of déjà vu. The grounds and buildings were almost a mirror copy of Butterface Winery. Ross Gregory had pretty much recreated the winery he'd sold.

The wine tasting room was still open, so I rode directly there.

Making my way to the entry, I exchanged nods with a young man and woman sitting on the deck, sipping white wine and enjoying the beautiful view of the quaint town spread out below the property. Though the building's shell looked similar to the one over at Butterface on the outside, inside it was very different. Crossing the threshold, it was as if I'd stepped through a portal into a different era. Frank Sinatra crooned a silky-smooth song in the background. Thick candles flickered on every horizontal surface adding ambiance to the natural light. Crushed velvet and dark stained oak on the massive bar and throughout the room contributed to the Fifties vibe.

A tall, slender man looking like he'd stepped right out of one the Rat Pack movies, in his old-style suit and jauntily-tilted Fedora, completed the transformation. He was busy pointing out all the awards, inside a glass trophycase, that Gregory Estates Wines had won over the years, to an older couple. Since there was only one car out front, I assumed the two couples were together. Judging by the age difference, these people were quite likely the parents of one of the two on the deck.

"I'll be right with you," the man in the hat called towards me.

"No rush," I replied, taking a seat at the fancy bar while he continued to extoll the virtues of Gregory Estate Wines.

A large framed photo hanging on the wall across from me was of a younger version of the hard-selling Fedora man, who was obviously Ross Gregory, cutting a ribbon at the opening ceremony of the building I sat in. In the crowd behind him I recognized several faces I'd seen earlier in the day, along with Milo and Mavis Getz.

The couple finally settled on a variety of six bottles, three red and three white. Buying six gave them a fifteen percent discount. A hundred and ninety-two dollars went on their Visa card. As they exited, Mr. Gregory approached holding two glasses of wine. As he got closer, I realized that he looked very much like Old Blue Eyes, albeit a much taller version of the famous singer.

"This one is on the house, for being so patient," he said, smiling warmly and holding out the glass of wine. "I don't sample this wine very often, but I've had a very good day." I'd turned down samples all afternoon, but decided to accept this one since this was my last interview today. Gregory lifted his glass toward the window light, gave it a swirl and then held it to his nose. I imitated his actions. "Note the dark color and the rich aroma, with some hints of cherry and plum, and just a suggestion of cocoa."

The cherry and plum were evident to me right away, but the cocoa took a deeper whiff.

"There's the cocoa," I agreed. Remembering my conversation with the Martins, I lowered my glass and took a guess. "Malbec?"

"Very good." He seemed very pleased and genuinely impressed. "You know your wine, Miss?"

"Swann, Reggie Swann," I watched for signs of recognition, but didn't see any.

"I'm very pleased to meet you, Reggie. I'm Ross Gregory, the owner of this establishment and purveyor of our fine wines." He raised his glass and then took in a mouthful, rolling it from one cheek to the other and back several times. Gregory's eyes were closed during his obviously well-practiced tasting ritual.

I took a sip and held it on my tongue. The cherry and plum flavoring gave the mellow wine just the right amount of fruitiness for my amateur pallet. I swallowed about the same time as he. I didn't notice the cocoa at all until the finish, but there it was. "This is really quite excellent."

"Thank you, thank you," Gregory said, beaming with pride. "I humbly happen to think it is the best Malbec ever produced in the region."

"I don't doubt it," I replied truthfully, then took another sip.

"Gregory Estates Reserve 2004," he told me, then guided me toward his trophy case and pointed to a blue ribbon. "Best New Wine, Canadian Food and Wine Institute."

"Very impressive," I told him, then knowing that he sold his former winery in 2006 I decided to push the conversation toward a more productive direction. "Then it came from your previous winery."

"Yes." He stepped back and took a closer look at my face. "Are you a critic? Have we met before?"

"No I'm not a critic, but it is possible we've met before. I grew up in the area," I told him, then took out one of my business cards and handed it to him. "I was hoping to speak to you about Milo Getz."

"Tragic accident, just terrible," he said, staring at my card as if the information on it didn't compute. "You're a private investigator?"

"That's right," I confirmed. "I'm talking to everyone who had recent contact with Mr. Getz."

"Why?"

"His wife, Mavis, hired me to look into his death."

"I thought the police said it was an accident," he said, as his eyes became furtive. He looked shaken.

"His widow doesn't think so." The twinge in my bones had returned in full force.

"I must get over there and convey my condolences," Gregory said, sinking into a nearby chair. "What makes her think it was anything but an accident?"

"She has her reasons," I said, sitting in a chair opposite him. "You were one of the last people to see him alive."

"Yes, I suppose so." Gregory stared into his glass. "Milo was fine when Terry Martin and I left. We left together, I might add."

"What time was that?" I asked, while making a show of taking out my notebook and pen. He watched carefully as I flipped it open and wrote his name atop a blank page.

"I don't know exactly, but it was pretty late."

"What time did you get home?"

"Again, I'm not sure." He shrugged.

"Maybe your wife would remember when you got back?"

"Normally she would, but we are separated. I came home to an empty house."

"I'm very sorry to hear that," I said, sympathetically. That would explain why he'd been at the party alone.

"Thank you."

"Terry Martin said that you hounded Milo for a sample of his new wine," I prodded.

"I might have," Gregory said, frowning. "Well yes, of course, I was curious about the new wine. He wouldn't budge, so I eventually let it go. It is no secret that I disliked what he had done to my winery, in the beginning. Throwing all my grapes together to make generic blends. I thought he was crazy or worse, but Milo surprised us all. Who can argue with the success of the Butterface label?"

"Weren't you envious of that success?"

"Milo made me a wealthy man," Ross Gregory countered. "Besides, if anyone has a reason to hold a grudge it might be Terry Martin. Losing a vintner the caliber of Roman was a loss he never fully recovered from. At one time, he used to sell more wine than I did. Crooked Branch had some damn good wines back then, not so much anymore. A particularly weak offering a few years back almost put them under. Rumor has it, that the Getz's stepped in to help just before the bank called in their loan."

Maybe I'd been hasty dismissing the Martins as suspects.

"Still, you weren't even a little jealous that Milo had become the largest bottler in the Okanagan?"

"I was proud of what he'd accomplished," Gregory stated. "Plus, I was thrilled to find out that Butterface would finally be offering some wines worthy of my old vineyard. I, better than anyone else, know the kind of grapes those fields are capable of growing."

"With Milo out of the way, who knows, maybe you can get your old winery back?"

"I'm happy where I am. The Summerland growers are a close knit family. It is quite gratifying to be part of this supportive community." He smiled and glanced around his lavish tasting room. "Besides, Mavis loves those vineyards as much as I did. She's not going anywhere."

"You sound like you know her well."

"We'd become friends over the years. That woman knows her grapes. After I sold the place, she and I met several times to discuss my old watering routines and the fertilizers I'd used. At first, I thought I was teaching her, but I eventually discovered she knew as much about the vines as I did, maybe more. We've continued to meet for coffee regularly over the years, and more recently, mostly for my benefit. She is a good friend. What she and Roman have accomplished is truly amazing." He got a faraway look in his eyes and then pointed at the photo I'd looked at earlier. "Mavis and Milo were honored guests at my grand opening five years ago, you know."

Mavis, maybe? But I wasn't convinced he'd changed his mind about Milo. I was about to ask him about the Malbec vines, but decided to try a different tactic. Some people loved to talk about their failed relationships, others not so much. I took the risk. "If you don't mind my asking, what happened between you and your wife, Mr. Gregory?" Immediately, I could tell from his body language that I'd hit a nerve.

"It's just a passing phase," he said, quietly, staring at the table top. "Vicki accused me of being stuck in the past." He set the Fedora on the table and rubbed his thinning scalp. He looked ten years older without the hat. "So what, if I don't play a guitar or wear tight leather pants?" Mr. Gregory shook his head, his eyes looking past me at a photo above the bar. I'd looked at it earlier, but this time I paid particular attention to Mrs. Gregory. She was staring at Milo like an awe-struck teen.

I returned my gaze to Gregory, his eyes were now shut and he was swaying, though barely perceptively, as Mel Torme's 'Blue Moon' filled the background. I glanced back at the photo and guessed that there was at least a fifteen-year age-span between the man and his wife. I knew better than most that ten or fifteen years could make for big changes in the world. For example, the Crooners had been replaced by Rock and Rollers.

"Was Mrs. Gregory a fan?"

"A fan?" he asked, his eyes opening slowly.

"Your wife, was she a fan of Milo's?" I nodded toward the photo, watching his face carefully. There it was, his lips tightened for a milli-second, then his face went completely blank. Anger or perhaps jealousy, I couldn't be certain which, but I'd seen something. "Milo's music, I mean."

"If you don't mind, I need to close up now." He stood and picked up our unfinished glasses. My senses were tingling, I'd definitely touched a nerve. I wanted to continue, but I could see he was finished talking.

"Thank you for your time and the tasting," I told him and headed toward the door.

"For your information," he said, as I was about to step back into the modern world. "That night, I gave Terry a ride home. Milo was alive and well when we left him. Check with Terry, he'll confirm it."

I nodded. That information jived with what the Martins had told me, as well.

The sun had dropped below the western horizon, but there was still lots of ambient light. I added Vicki Gregory's name onto my 'To Interview' list, before getting on Betsy. As I rode away, I felt sorry for Ross Gregory – he obviously still loved his old vineyard and his wife. It was possible he'd lost them both to Milo Getz. The Martins hadn't mentioned that the Gregorys were separated; of course, they also hadn't mentioned their bank troubles or Milo's intervention. Did the Martin's owe Milo money? I finally had some actual suspects. Well, suspects might be a strong word, but I definitely had persons of interest. I'd take a much closer look at the Martins, and Mr. Rat Pack and his estranged wife, Vicki. Money, jealousy and unrequited love were all excellent motives.

Surprise, surprise, Mom was out with friends when I got home. She'd thoughtfully left a Saran-wrapped plate of roasted chicken and assorted vegetables in the fridge for me. While it warmed in the microwave, I left a message on Hannah's home phone pushing our get-together back twenty-four hours. I'd planned to meet with her later, to compare notes, but I didn't have much to share and I wanted to finish going through the videos that Roman had provided. Alan and a few of his guy friends were in Kelowna to catch an Okanagan Sun game so I had the evening to myself.

Being the fun-loving gal that I am, I grabbed my plate of reheated food, popped the third of the four Butterface security camera DVDs into the DVR and settled in front of Mom's Samsung. The colorful screen came to life. The resolution was very good. I immediately recognized several of the faces I'd seen earlier today. The picture was so crisp and clear compared to most of the business surveillance tapes I used to go through when I was a cop. Often black and white, almost always fuzzy, even after the techs did their best to clean it up.

This wasn't the most riveting reality TV. However, I did perk up when I spotted Damien Eberle speaking to a tall, dark-haired man. I looked at the time code: 08:36. This must be the fellow he had described in our interview. I couldn't get a good look at the stranger's face from this angle. At 08:37 the man simply turned and walked away. He appeared to have hardly acknowledged Damien's presence the entire time the smaller man had spoken to him. I rewound the tape and watched the exchange again. The man had absently shaken Damien's offered hand, but his focus was elsewhere. I hit pause and stood up.

DVD 1 was the camera in the southwest corner, it would offer the best angle of the man's face. I grabbed the disc and headed up to my room, to use my laptop. I'd be able to zoom in and print off screen captures. My new found technical skills were owed entirely to Rhonda. I'd still be completely analogue if it hadn't been for her patient help.

I fast forwarded to 08:30 and dropped back to real time. There was the intense, dark stranger in the middle of the room standing perfectly still while the other party-goers gaily shuffled past and around him, as though he were a living statue. Comparing him to those nearby, he was a big fellow, heavyset in a physical/muscular sort of way. Despite a slightly protruding gut, the man looked like he could handle himself. I estimated he was in the back half of middle-age, late forties or very early fifties. Something or someone definitely had his attention. I zoomed in until his face filled the screen. That was a nose that had been broken more than once. His mouth and jaw were locked in a neutral position, but he couldn't hide the fire in those dark, almost black eyes. If looks could kill...

After being still for so long, his head suddenly bobbed to the side, then settled back into place. I glanced at the time code: 08:36. I zoomed out. There was Damien Eberle, a full head shorter than my unknown subject, chatting away, but getting no response in return. I watched until the man turned and walked away, then reversed back and took a few screen shots of my new suspect and printed them off, to show Hannah. If the guy was in the system, she'd get an ID.

Curiosity got the better of me. I needed to know what or who the man was staring at. I popped open the DVD drawer and swapped in disc #3 which would provide the opposite view. I suspected that I'd see Milo at the other end of his stare, but I was wrong. Off to the unsub's right, the musician/winery owner and a few others were exiting the building.

If Milo wasn't the object of his rage, maybe the mysterious man wasn't a suspect after all. I zoomed past the stranger, all the way to the opposite wall. I remembered that particular piece of wall from my visit to the tasting room. It was dedicated to Milo's and Aurora's biggest success, their 'Butterface' album. Gold and platinum plaques flanked an oversized copy of the album cover. Framed newspaper and magazine articles filled in the area below, detailing its virtues. Everything you wanted to know about the album and its songs was there on the wall, I knew from reading every word.

I'd been surprised to learn that The Tragically Hip and Nickelback were the only Canadian Bands to have sold more albums worldwide than Aurora. I'd been even more surprised to discover that Michael Buble had outsold these three bands. Celine and Shania, sure, but Michael? There had also been a scathing article from a 2004 issue of Rolling Stone claiming Aurora, their album 'Butterface' and its number one single -- 'Two Bagger', should have won multiple Grammys that year but were shut out due to politics. The fans had spoken the loudest by making 'Butterface' the number-one-selling album worldwide for three consecutive months after the Grammys.

I grabbed the photos from the printer and held the closeup of the mystery man's face next to the monitor. The eyes don't lie. This guy was not a fan, that much was certain.

Next, I pulled the focus of the screen back from the wall, to the unsub, and hit rewind. For just over five minutes the back of his head barely moved, even while Mr. Eberle spoke to him. Finally, he began to walk backwards. I was able to follow his movements, through the crowd, back to his arrival inside the tasting room. The timecode read: 08:29:44. I loaded another DVD to get a better look at him and cued it up to 08:29:40, zoomed in to the entryway and let it play at real time.

When the unsub stepped through the door, he paused and looked around. He spotted Milo near the bar. There was the hatred again. He quickly looked away though. As he wandered through milling people, paying them no mind, his focus appeared to be on the building structure itself. He paid particular attention to the heavily beamed ceiling and then checked out the wood floor. He was surveying the walls when he spotted the album display. He stopped in his tracks, his body went rigid and he turned into the living statue I'd witnessed from just about every angle. The scene was surreal. I watched it again with fascination. The party continued around him, but he did not flinch once until Mr. Eberle walked over and introduced himself. Even then, his eyes barely left the wall. A few seconds after the absent-minded handshake, it was as if the unsub woke from a trance. I zoomed in further and went back a few seconds and watched that part again. I hadn't noticed that before. Tears had gathered in the corners of his eyes. I watched as the sudden look of disorientation struck. The eyes finally left the wall, glanced wildly around before settling on the small man in front of him. The unsub forced a nod and then shortly afterward retreated to the exit.

I checked my watch. As often happened, time had flown by while I worked. Never-the-less, I was genuinely surprised to see that midnight had come and gone a while back. I shut down my laptop. It had been a productive day. I now had people of interest in the Milo Getz murder investigation. The Martins had withheld their debt to Milo, I needed to find out why. Something seemed off about Ross Gregory. I couldn't put my finger on what, though maybe a chat with his estranged wife would shed some light. Of course, the mysterious stranger now trumped them all as my best suspect.

As I retrieved the baton from my pocket and removed the magazines from my forearms, my thoughts returned to the stalker. Was he or she just another newspaper reporter gathering background information? I chased away the idea that there may be another serial killer lurking around the Okanagan. I sincerely hoped it was just an overly zealous journalist. I needed to know who was watching me, and why. Though I didn't feel eyes on me now, I walked to the window and surveyed up and down the street. Nothing looked unusual. I shut out the lights and settled into bed as a rough plan to catch my stalker started to form.

CHAPTER 17

I rolled out of bed, excited and a little nervous about the basement renovation. We would be doing the walk-through/big reveal with Buck this morning. Just like some of the HGTV programs that Mom had introduced me to, I hadn't been allowed to see the progress for the past week, when all the cool stuff like flooring, cabinets, lights and paint was being installed or applied. Mom's idea. She hadn't been down there either. It had been a group design and decorating project, with ideas and suggestions from Mom, Hannah, Rhonda, Erika and, of course, Buck. Thank goodness, without their guidance the process would have been overwhelming for me. There were too many choices. I couldn't have done it alone. They'd made the project fun. I couldn't wait to see how it all turned out.

But first, I had my morning ritual to do. After brushing my teeth, I dropped to the floor and began with pushups. It had been a matter of survival once, now my routine was as much a security blanket like strapping magazines to my forearms. I occasionally go to Alan's gym with him, but not to do my morning workout anymore. That first morning, as I proceeded with my exercise regime, in which the only fitness equipment I use is the floor, a small section of wall, a door frame and a chair, a crowd soon formed as I did one-armed pushups, single-legged squats, etc. I don't much like crowds, even when they're gasping at or applauding my fitness efforts. Plus, Alan spends a lot of money purchasing and maintaining high quality fitness apparatus. My choosing to use a chair for dips or a door frame for chin-ups rather than the nearby fancy machines hadn't exactly been the best promotion for his business. We'd agreed that my morning workouts were best done at home.

Partway through my run, I felt eyes on me once again. Giving up the pretense of being unaware of their presence, I openly searched the roads, vineyards and orchards for signs of my stalker. I came up empty, but I knew they were out there.

After a shower and then breakfast with Mom, Hannah's unmarked cruiser pulled into the driveway next to Buck's huge GMC pickup truck. She'd picked up Erika and Rhonda. The gang was all here. It was time to see my new place. I was about to run into the house and get Mom, but she was already coming through the garage toward us. We marched down the new sidewalk to the newly added lower entrance and rang the new doorbell.

Buck stuck his head out the door, annoyingly shielding the interior with his long body. "Good morning, ladies."

"Good morning, Buck," we shouted, almost in unison.

"By gosh, just look at all of you. Covergirl magazine must be doing a shoot here this morning."

"More like Farmer's Journal," Erika quickly responded.

"Hey, I resent that," Rhonda piped up. "I was raised on a farm."

"I know..."

After some laughter and an insincere apology from Erika, Mom said what we were all thinking. "Are you ever going to let us inside?" Buck smiled at her then turned to me.

"First, close yer eyes, Reggie girl," he said mischievously, in his charming Aussie accent. "No peaking 'til you're all the way in."

"I'll make sure," Hannah said from behind me and her fingers slid around my head and locked in front of my face. We shuffled forward. "Threshold," Hannah whispered. I probably lifted my feet high enough to step over a laundry basket. But at least I didn't trip.

There were several oohs and ahs around me before Hannah finally removed her hands. I'd pictured these rooms in my mind, but the reality proved to be much better.

"Better Homes and Gardens," I said, my voice breaking. My eyes welled up with tears of joy. I'd had doubts about the chocolate-milkshake-colored walls, but they were gorgeous. Wide white baseboards and trim really made them pop.

"This does not seem like a basement," Erika stated, reading my mind. "It's so bright and filled with light."

"We did a little excavating in the back yard so that we could add larger windows," Buck replied.

"Well it was definitely worth it," she added. "You did a fantastic job."

Everyone began to wander, but I was too stunned to move. The whole space, including the bedroom suite, which I hadn't seen yet, was only 850 square feet. Yet, to me, the place looked huge. I know that I'm accustomed to small spaces, but this looked larger than it should.

Buck stepped in front of me. "Is everything okay, Darlin'?"

"More than okay," I told him, trying not to cry. "It is more spacious than I was expecting."

Buck smiled and pointed over his head. "Remember the pipe that was here?"

I looked upward. There was nothing there. The hanging pipes hadn't been framed and covered with drywall, they were gone altogether.

"I was able to reroute all the ducting into the floor joists and make the entire ceiling eight feet high."

"Well, whatever it cost, it was worth it," I said, borrowing Erika's recent comment.

"Nothing," Buck said.

"It can't have been nothing," I told him. "That must have been a lot of work."

Buck shrugged, "It was my house-warming gift to my favorite client."

"Thank you, Buck," I said, as I threw my arms around him. "You didn't have to do that."

"I wanted to." Buck squeezed me back, before wiping away a tear of his own. "Speaking of house-warming gifts, the girls have something to show you."

Everyone had a smirk on their faces.

"You guys..."

They led me to the bedroom. It should have been empty, but it wasn't.

"Wha-what is all this?" I stammered.

"Surprise," they shouted in unison.

I'd planned to move most of my old bedroom furniture from upstairs into the new space. Not now. My new bedroom was fully furnished. I stepped into the room and spun around to take it all in. Sheer black curtains had been added to the slatted window blinds. The gorgeous black-stained six-drawer dresser, tall credenza and night stands were the supporting cast for the star attraction: a king-sized bed. The ornate quilt covering the bed, featured a graceful black swan just about to land on a serene marsh pond. The detail was incredible, from the individual feathers to the cattail reeds. The closer you looked the more impressive it became. How these tiny multi-colored squares, sewn together, formed such an intricate mosaic was a mystery I'd never solve. I leaned forward, reached my hand towards it. I hesitated, afraid it all might vanish if I touched it. It was real, I hadn't dreamed all this. A closer look revealed that the stitching incorporated a tiny swan replicated over each and every square. I'd never seen anything like it in my life. The quilt was magnificent, beyond words. The bedroom set was perfect, better than perfect, if that is possible. Of course, anything is better than a prison cell, but this... Tears filled my eyes.

"Do you like it?" Somebody asked, breaking the hypnotic state I'd slipped into.

I turned around and opened my mouth but nothing came out. All I could do was nod my head up and down emphatically. After a group hug, I managed to find my voice.

"Thank you, thank you, you shouldn't have," I told them, as I sat back against the edge of the bed. The mattress felt firm, they'd even gotten that right. I'd had to put a sheet of plywood under my mattress upstairs to make it firm enough to be comfortable. Ten years on a prison cot had changed my taste in bed comfort. "This is all just so perfect."

"We knew frilly wasn't your style," Hannah pointed out.

"Where did you find this amazing quilt?" I asked. All the faces turned toward Mom. "You did this?"

"Oh heavens, no." Mom laughed. "Do you remember Lisa Brownley?" I guess the blank look on my face answered that question. "Chelsey Ann's mother?"

Chelsey Ann I remembered from my high school days, then Mrs. Brownley's cheerful face came to me. "From Okanagan Falls, right?"

"That's correct," Mom confirmed. "Lisa's a big-time quilter. Her work wins contests and awards all over the province."

"I can see why," I said, running my hand back and forth across the soft surface.

"I suggested the black swan theme and Lisa did the rest."

"I hate to break up the party, but I have to get to work," Hannah interjected.

"Yes," Erika added. "Some of us have schedules and appointments."

"You guys should try retirement," Mom chuckled. "It's wonderful, I could go back to bed if I wanted." This was met with a round of envious groans. "I'm not going to, but I could."

"Quit rubbing it in," Hannah said, "or I might have to arrest you."

"On what charge?" Mom challenged.

"Cruel and inhumane treatment of us working stiffs," Rhonda retorted, causing a round of laughter.

"My apologies ladies," Mom said.

"Apology accepted, Madam," Buck immediately answered, pretending to hold a skirt hem out to his sides as he curtsied. This caused a roar of laughter.

"Ladies and gentleman," Mom corrected.

I tugged Rhonda's sleeve and asked her to stay behind as the group filed out the door and headed back toward the front of the house. I followed and saw them off. As soon as the driveway cleared Mom drove away, too. Friday mornings she has coffee with a group of her friends, all widowed or divorced. A couple of them have remarried, but they still get together every week. When Dad passed, they'd been there for Mom when I couldn't be. I'd be forever grateful for that.

CHAPTER 18

From the living room window, it felt a little surreal as a reasonable facsimile of myself rode off on Betsy. Rhonda and I are about the same height. Her hair is longer and darker than mine, but it was tucked away under my helmet.

As I'd gotten to know Rhonda better, I'd discovered that the girl underneath the perfect makeup and wrinkle-free clothes was not afraid to get dirt under those manicured fingernails. I'd been surprised to witness the supremely capable and competent Legal Assistant become a fun-loving and fearless force outside of office hours. Raised on a farm, the only girl in a family with three older brothers, Rhonda learned to keep up with the boys or get left behind. I don't know why but it had shocked me to learn that she'd been riding and racing dirtbikes since she was twelve.

A few minutes earlier, after I'd explained my plan to her, Rhonda gamely swapped her skirt and blouse for the khaki pants and cotton blouse I'd been wearing. It was my typical garb for interviewing witnesses and I'd purposely worn the loosest fitting navy shirt that I had. It would best camouflage Rhonda's slightly narrower shoulders and two-size larger boobs. Earlier,

I'd spent some time in the front driveway slowly wiping the barely accumulated dust from Betsy's frame and cowl purposely giving my stalker a good chance to observe my outfit. After donning the goggles and helmet, Rhonda would have fooled my mother.

I rushed upstairs, grabbed my baton and pepper spray, attached a pair of magazines to my forearms and tucked a couple pairs of zip cuffs into my back pockets. Then I rushed back into the garage, pushed my bike through the side door, road up the alley, then flew down Vancouver Avenue, zipped through the roundabout taking Front Street to Main.

I chained my bike to a tree and checked my watch. I'd made good time. The stores weren't open yet, so the sidewalks weren't busy as I walked a block ahead to get into position. I got a small coffee, grabbed a free newspaper from Blenz Coffee and wandered further up the block to an empty bench and settled onto it, trying to look comfortable and uninterested in the world around me. It was not easy. I was using one of my few good friends as bait. Several bad scenarios played through my mind. If Rhonda got hurt, I'd never forgive myself.

It was a simple plan, but still... To give me time to get into place and keeping in character, Rhonda would ride to the office, go in my private entrance, wait ten minutes then lead our stalker here.

I breathed a sigh of relief as Betsy and Rhonda rolled around the corner, half a block away and across the street from my position. She pulled Betsy over and parked her.

Beyond them, a blue sedan pulled slowly through the intersection without turning. I was close enough this time to see that it was a late model BMW. I couldn't make out the driver through the tinted glass. I tugged down on the baseball cap I was wearing, to help hide my face.

There was still a half hour before the meters needed to be plugged. Rhonda got off the bike and without removing the helmet she walked quickly up the street toward me and then abruptly turned right and disappeared down a narrow, covered walkway just as we'd planned.

A figure jogged across the intersection walkway. It was a woman. I had to turn away as she came my way, so I didn't get a look at her face, but something about her movement seemed familiar.

As soon as the woman turned into the breezeway, I leapt to my feet and followed.

I'd instructed Rhonda to run as fast as she could once she got into the covered breezeway, circle the block and wait for me at the coffee shop.

"What if you need help?" she'd asked, not liking the idea.

"Wait ten minutes," I'd instructed, "if you don't see me call 911."

"I'll circle the block, but then I'm coming to find you," she'd said, then interrupted me as I opened my mouth to argue the point. "No discussion."

Seeing the fierce determination in her eyes, I'd reluctantly agreed.

I entered the west end of the tunnel, snapping open my baton as I ran into the darkness. At the far end, framed in the morning light, was the shadowy figure who'd been tailing me for at least three days. As she reached the east end, I could see her look right, then left. Her arms suddenly raised in frustration.

"Good girl, Rhonda," I whispered, as I achieved full sprint speed. There was thirty meters between us as the figure hesitated, deciding which way to go. The smart move was to her right. It would take her back to her car, where she could wait for me to return to Betsy.

She took a resigned step in the direction of her car. I'd covered two thirds of the distance, when my foot kicked a loose stone. It careened loudly off the wall. She stopped midstride and peered into the darkness. I lowered my shoulder and without slowing I rammed into her. I heard a surprised gasp as the air spewed from her lungs. We landed in a heap, skidding across the gravel alley. I was on top of the facedown woman. She bucked and twisted hard. I wasn't about to give up my advantage. I managed to get my knee jammed into the small of her back and my free hand on the back of her neck. I pressed down with all my weight.

"Stop moving," I shouted. She squirmed for a couple more seconds, before stopping. Then I felt a convulsion ripple through her.

"Can't bree," a desperate raspy voice sputtered.

"Don't try anything," I warned. Baton at the ready and adrenalin super-charging every cell in my body, I slid my knee off her back and eased the pressure on her neck. I lightly tapped the side of her head with the metal baton to remind her who was in charge.

"Ple-ea-se," she sputtered, still struggling to regain her breath. I felt her body convulse a couple more times beneath me, then she finally sucked in some air. She took in another long breath calming her oxygen-starved body, then surprised me by chuckling as she spoke again. "I guess the jig is up."

I recognized the voice. It couldn't be. My mind swirled with images of our last encounter. It had been in prison.

"I'm not here to fight with you, Blackie," she said, her familiar brown eyes staring up at the baton poised above her head.

She slowly laid her arms out submissively. There on the left cheek of her face was the small, but unmistakable, scar I'd given her during our first prison fight. Her mischievous smile was probably cute to her friends, but I'd been a sworn enemy. It usually meant trouble when aimed at me.

"Laynie?" I asked, trying to grasp why or even how it was possible she was here. The baton stayed where it was. "I don't understand."

"I'm out."

"Did you escape?"

"No, I'm on parole."

"Come on," I demanded, shaking the baton in a threatening manner.

"It's true."

"You were in for murder," I reminded her.

"That was a lie," Laynie sheepishly admitted. "Grand larceny. I convinced everyone I was in for murder to sound tougher."

She'd fooled me. I'd believed she was a lifer, like me. Lifers had almost nothing to lose; you generally didn't mess with a lifer unless you had a serious beef. Unfortunately, in my case, just about everyone had had a beef with me. Though none more than Laynie. The scar I stared down at was proof enough of that.

"What are you doing here?" I asked, still completely confused by her presence.

"To learn from the master."

"What the hell is that supposed to mean?"

"You're kind of my…" she hesitated, "my hero."

I couldn't help the doubtful look on my face.

"No, really," she insisted. "You're everyone's hero, man, especially at the farm." 'Farm' was a nickname some of the inmates had for prison.

"You, they, everyone hated me."

"You were a lifer and you got out," she said. "Inside, that is the stuff of dreams, man."

I was dumbfounded.

"Then when we found out that you told the Chief of Police and the Mayor to shove their job offer up their asses, you should have heard the cheering. The entire prison went nuts."

"That's not exactly what happened," I countered, recalling the day that I decided to stay in the Okanagan, with Mom and my true friends, rather than returning to Toronto and the people who'd been so quick to abandon me.

"It was like a switch had been thrown or something. You were no longer one of them, you became one of us that day," she explained. "You turned into a legend - the toughest bitch any of us ever met."

I heard feet skidding to a halt behind me.

"Are you okay?" Rhonda asked.

I looked into Laynie's eyes. There was no malice evident.

"Everything is fine, I think," I said, then with the baton still raised I asked the woman below me, "Any weapons on you?"

"That would be a parole violation," Laynie answered. I stared her down until she shrugged and pointed to her right calf. I slid my hand under the loose pant leg and found a knife strapped just above her ankle.

Laynie shrugged, as I handed the knife to Rhonda. "Purely for protection."

"Is that everything?"

Laynie nodded. I lifted myself off my sworn enemy's torso. We both stood. I had the baton ready.

"How did you manage to get the drop on me like that?" Laynie asked then chuckled again, noticing at the helmet in Rhonda's hand. "Slick move. I thought I was getting pretty good at this see without being seen thing. When did you figure out I was watching you?"

"Three days ago."

"Damn," Laynie frowned and shook her head.

"I couldn't see you, but I knew you were there," I admitted.

"Alright," she responded cheerfully. "That's not so bad."

"Reggie, just what the hell is going on?" Rhonda demanded, as Laynie got her feet. "Who is this woman and why has she been following you?"

"I'm sorry, Rhonda," I apologized. "I know who she is but I have no idea what she's doing here. Her name is Laynie Garcia..."

"We were friends in prison," Laynie interrupted and held out her hand toward Rhonda.

"Friends?" The word burst forth through my lips. "You tried to kill me -- twice."

Rhonda leaned menacingly toward Laynie, readying both the knife and my cherry red helmet for an attack.

"She tried to kill you?"

"No, no, I never wanted to kill Reggie," Laynie replied nonchalantly.

That was the first time, I'd ever heard her say my actual name. I'd been Blackie, Bitch Cop, Miss Piggy or something much worse. Never once in the nearly two years we'd done time together had she ever called me anything that hadn't been inflammatory.

Laynie's eyes locked onto mine. "I just meant to put you in the infirmary, is all. I told you I'm not a killer, just a thief. I mean I was a thief. Not a thief anymore, really, those days are behind me. I know what I want to do with my life, thanks to you."

Rhonda set down my helmet and took out her phone. "I'm calling the police. I work for a lawyer..."

"White, Garrison and White," Laynie interrupted, not helping her cause.

"I'm pretty certain that stalking is a parole violation and this certainly is," Rhonda said, shaking the knife in Laynie's direction.

"Wait, please," Laynie pleaded. "I wasn't stalking, I was practicing my surveillance technique."

"It's ringing," Rhonda reported.

"I'm telling the truth, you've got to believe me." Laynie's voice had a desperate edge now. "I'm like... What's the word? ... an apprentice! That's it. I'm your apprentice."

"You're not my apprentice." I was still trying to wrap my head around her presence. The last time I'd seen her, Laynie vowed to kill me as she was being dragged by a prison guard toward a ten-day stint in the hole.

Standing next to each other, I suddenly realized Rhonda, wearing my clothes, and Laynie were dressed almost identically. Laynie was wearing khakis and a pale blue long sleeve cotton blouse. Her hair, though much darker than mine, was cut to the same length and style as my own. Laynie had copied my look right down to the shoes, rubber-soled, low-heeled pumps. They were comfortable and you could run in them, if needed. In fact, as I looked closer, they were an exact match to the ones on my feet. I'd just bought these two days ago. A shoe sale at Ronson's in Kelowna that Erika had dragged me to.

"Wait," I told Rhonda. "Hang up."

"You're not buying her BS?"

"I want to hear her out," I said. "The benefit of the doubt and all that."

161

CHAPTER 19

"**Y**ou don't have to stay," I told Rhonda, as the three of us settled into a booth, back at the coffee shop.

"I'm not going anywhere," she said, her finger poised above her phone's send button. I recognized the number on the screen as Hannah's direct line. "If I hear or see anything, and I mean anything, I don't like, she's going back to prison."

Laynie sat across from us, her back to the rear wall, where I'd have been if I'd gotten there first. I still didn't like turning my back on people. I glanced behind me at the next booth. An old man, in his late seventies or early eighties, was reading the paper while ignoring his wife, of the same vintage, as she reminded him that they needed to hire someone to clear the leaves from the eave-troughs. He grunted in response. They looked harmless. I relaxed a little and scanned the rest of the room for possible threats.

"Start talking," Rhonda commanded, crossing her arms. It was a little heartwarming to see her so protective of me.

"What do you want to know?" Laynie asked, taking a sip from her steaming mug. She'd changed her order from a black coffee to a hot chocolate, after I'd ordered one.

"Laynie, why are you here?" I asked. Now that the adrenalin rush had subsided I felt even more confused by her presence.

"Honestly, I first thought about becoming a bounty hunter."

"There are no bounty hunters in Canada," Rhonda and I said in unison.

"Or bail bondsmen," Laynie added. "Yeah, I quickly found that out. Then I decided I'd become a Private Dick, just like you, Reggie."

"Do you have any law enforcement training?" Rhonda sneered, while I tried to make sense of the words that had just come out of Laynie's mouth.

"I've studied the subject," Laynie said.

"At an accredited school?" Rhonda queried.

"Maybe, I didn't check the credentials..." She could see that Rhonda wasn't at all impressed by her answer. "But, you know what they say?"

"Enlighten me." Rhonda uncrossed her arms, finger once again hovering above her phone.

"Sometimes it takes a criminal to catch a criminal."

"It takes a thief to catch a thief," I corrected her.

"You see," Laynie gloated.

"Why are you here, in Penticton?" I demanded, more forcefully than I meant to.

"Because of you, Blackie."

"Blackie?" Rhonda shrugged.

"That's what they called me in prison," I told her. She glanced at my light brown hair and shrugged again. "Short for Black Swann."

"Oh," she said, then glared at Laynie. "That wasn't very nice."

"Actually, that was the nicest thing they called me inside."

"No doubt," Laynie laughed. "We mostly called you Miss Piggy or Pig Bi..."

"I had a lot of nicknames," I said, cutting her off for Rhonda's benefit. "Let's get back to why you are here."

"Where should I start?"

"How about at the beginning," I suggested. There was something different about Laynie, and it wasn't just her clothes. There was a positive vibe I'd never seen before. The tough-guy façade, she'd carried around the prison, was gone. There was still an edginess to her, but all the false bravado had been replaced with smiles. That's what it was, I'd never seen a genuine smile on her face before. Laynie Garcia was actually a pleasant looking human being. I was shocked.

"The beginning, okay. It's actually a pretty good story," Laynie said, smiling broadly. She had nice looking teeth when she wasn't sneering.

"When I got out of the hole..."

"Solitary confinement," I added for Rhonda's benefit.

"...Everything had changed, man." She shook her head. "It was like I'd stepped into an alternate universe or something. Same building, same people, but it was all different."

"Different how?" I wondered aloud. Ten years of my life bounced around in my head, none of it good.

"The whole atmosphere had changed," Laynie said. "And for the better."

"How?" I asked, trying to imagine a positive change inside those droll walls.

"The whole place was different because of you," Laynie chuckled. "When I went in the hole, you were the most hated person inside." She paused, then looked me in the eyes. "When I came out, you were like, I don't know, Wonder Woman."

"What are you talking about?" I stammered.

"The indestructible Black Swann," she said, with some awe in her voice. "You'd become a hero, a legend. The amazing woman who took everything we threw at her and spit it back in our faces. The lifer, the inmate without possibility of parole was out in the world walking free."

"Wow," Rhonda exclaimed. I was too taken aback by Laynie's words to speak. I'd never imagined my release would have any impact on the prison.

"Your story united us," Laynie told me directly. "That the badass Black Swann had beaten us and the system were the two things that everyone could agree upon."

"Okay, let's get to the part about why you are here," I said, feeling uncomfortable.

"No, go on, I want to hear about this," Rhonda countermanded.

"Our scars," she said, running her finger along the thin white line across her cheek bone, "became badges of honor."

"Reggie did that to you?" Rhonda asked, glancing back and forth between us.

"Oh, yeah, quite a number of us had these little reminders of what happens when you take a run at the Black Swann," Laynie laughed. "We deserved them; I know I did. This one was from our first encounter. I'd despised this beauty, up until that day."

"I was just protecting myself," I fibbed to Rhonda. The truth was, I had taken a perverse pleasure in seeing the scars and injuries I'd administered to those who'd come at me. Outsiders, would never completely understand the dynamics of prison life, especially the life of a cop in prison. Even still, I was no longer proud of my behavior back then.

"Funny thing," Laynie said, her voice serious, "when I told everyone the story about the last beating you gave me and how I'd cut you but you didn't bleed, your legend grew and I suddenly had the respect I thought only beating you would bring me."

"Do you have a scar from the second fight, too?" Rhonda asked Laynie. She really seemed to be getting into the account of our time behind bars together. I'd played down how tough my life had been in prison, to my friends. Hannah had some idea and, of course, Mom had seen me in the infirmary on more than one occasion, so she knew some of what had gone on. But no one outside those walls really knew what it had been like for a cop in prison, save for maybe the woman in front of us.

"I wish," Laynie replied, then turned her attention to me. "But you should have had one. I can't figure out how you pulled that off. I know that I cut your arm. Laynie turned back to Rhonda, "I cut her wrist, but when the guard checked her for a wound it wasn't there."

"Things were happening pretty fast," I explained to both of them.

"Not that fast," Laynie shook her head. "I felt the blade bite into your arm, Wonder Woman."

"I'm not Wonder Woman, if you cut me I bleed," I said, remembering the day I lost my kidney and almost my life. "You just thought you cut me."

"I know I did," Laynie countered.

I put my arm on the table in front of her and slowly unbuttoned the cuff of my sleeve. Both Laynie and Rhonda held their breath as I tugged the sleeve up my forearm, exposing the magazine wrapped around it. After a few seconds of stunned silence, Laynie began to laugh. Rhonda joined in.

"I thought, for a second, you were going to show us your golden bracelets, Wonder Woman," Laynie said.

"Me, too," Rhonda said. "But somehow this is even better."

"I'm not Wonder Woman," I protested.

"Maybe not," Rhonda said, "but you are the Black Swann."

I searched for a rebuttal. Before anything came to me, my former mortal enemy slammed her fist on the table.

"You always wore sweatshirts," Laynie gasped, as her laughter settled down to a chuckle. "Even during the summer." She picked up a butter knife and held it above my arm. "Do you mind?"

I shrugged an approval. Laynie closed her eyes and ran the dull blade firmly across the magazine, cutting and tearing through four or five pages, but getting nowhere near my skin. Her eyes flashed open. She looked down at the magazine, then a huge smile spread across her face. "There is so much I can learn from you, Black Swann."

"I'm not a super hero," I protested.

"You kind of are, Reggie," Rhonda pointed out.

"I don't know anyone else who could have survived what you did. No normal person that's for certain," Laynie confirmed. "I know another 250 women in Kingston who would say the same thing."

I didn't know what to say. They were both staring at me strangely. I started to feel even more uncomfortable. I'm not shy, but I've never liked being the center of attention. Thankfully, Laynie broke the awkward silence. Though, the next words that came out of her mouth stunned me further.

"You should go back to Kingston for a visit."

Why on earth would I ever go back to that place? The thought was inconceivable.

"The girls would love to see you," Laynie continued, though her words made no sense to me. "You could give a talk or maybe do a book signing. Like I said, you are their hero."

A chill ran down my spine at the thought of ever stepping foot again into the horrible hellhole that had devoured a significant chunk of my life. "I could never..." I sputtered, as my stomach did flip-flops. I suddenly remembered how it felt to be surrounded by concrete and iron bars and the dread I'd lived with on a daily basis with possible threats waiting around every corner, behind each doorway, within the dark shadows. "...go back to that place."

Rhonda noticed my discomfort.

"Are you okay?" she asked, putting her hand on my shoulder.

"Sorry, I'm fine," I assured, adding a smile. Her touch reminding me that I was amongst friends, mostly. I peeked over my shoulder to confirm that the couple behind us wasn't plotting my demise, then turned my attention back to the woman across the table.

"It was just a thought," Laynie said, with a shrug.

"Let's get back to why you are here," I said, gathering myself. I had pushed the fear, despair and frustration that had once been a regular part of my daily life into the dark recesses of my mind. I was surprised at how easily those demons could rear their ugly heads. They slowly slithered back into the darkness.

Laynie spent half an hour explaining how my exploits in the media had inspired her. She knew what she wanted to do with the rest of her life. Laynie Garcia was going to be a private investigator just like the Black Swann. Heaven help us. She'd gotten into fitness. When she did get out, she hadn't gone back to her old neighborhood where she'd have ended up hanging around with her hoodlum buddies. Laynie had taken every online criminology course she could get her hands on and had read my book several times.

"And how did you manage to get out so soon?" I asked.

"That part was easy." She smiled at us. "I ratted out my no-good-for-nothing, lousy, lying, cheating, boyfriend, that's how."

Rhonda looked confused.

"I'm pretty good at boosting cars," Laynie explained. "I mean that I used to be. Jimmy, the rat-bastard, was even better at moving them. Most of the cars were chopped for parts, a few were sanitized and flipped locally."

"Sanitized?" I interrupted.

"New VIN, adjust the odometer, throw on a coat of paint, replace the wheels and even the former owner wouldn't recognize the car," Laynie said, shrugging. "And the really high-end rides were packed up and shipped out of the country."

"And you were a part of this theft ring?" Rhonda asked.

"A big part," Laynie responded, with more than a hint of pride. "I did the books."

"I thought you were a car thief?" I questioned her.

"I was at the start and then at the end," Laynie shrugged. "You see, in the beginning it was just Jimmy and me. I stole 'em and he chopped 'em," she explained. "We had a sweet little business going, but we got greedy. At the height of our business we had ten guys boosting cars for us in four different cities. Cars were coming and going; cash was flooding in. Someone had to keep track of it all, and that job fell to me. By the end, I was carrying a briefcase to work every morning. Can you believe that?"

I was definitely struggling to picture the Laynie Garcia I had known in prison as a business woman.

"So how did you get caught?" Rhonda asked, quite possibly saving my head from exploding.

"A Phantom," Laynie chuckled, cheerfully.

"You were caught by a phantom." Rhonda stated, heavy on the sarcasm. Her eyes turned to mine. I could see she was starting to like my sworn enemy.

"A Rolls-Royce Phantom..." Laynie went on to explain how the RCMP had set up a sting operation. A wealthy customer made a request and, low and behold, she came across the exact car he was looking for on her way work the very next morning. "I couldn't resist." Of course, the car had been a set up. The police nabbed her red-handed. Through all the interrogations and trial she'd refused to give up her partner. Until recently, when she discovered he'd been cheating on her, and had been even before she'd gone to prison.

"In exchange for an early release, I gave up the entire operation," Laynie admitted. "And now I've turned over a new leaf. I want to be just like you."

"You're driving a pretty nice car," I mentioned, with a strong hint of accusation in my voice.

"I didn't steal it," Laynie protested. "I promise."

"Pinky swear?" I asked sarcastically, the disbelief evident in my face. "Where did you get the money for a car like that?" I knew she hadn't gotten a loan. When I got out of prison my credit rating was gone, as if I'd never existed. I couldn't even get a cellphone without Mom's assistance.

"I'd rather not say."

I reached over and lowered my finger toward Rhonda's phone.

"Okay, okay," Laynie cried out. "I got a book deal with your publisher."

"Does everyone in prison automatically get a book deal?" Rhonda sputtered, looking back and forth between us.

"You sold them your story?" I asked Laynie, though I was pretty certain I already knew the answer.

"Not exactly," Laynie said sheepishly.

"What does that mean?" Rhonda asked.

"Until recently, my publisher had been hounding me to write a book about my life in prison." I said, staring into Laynie's eyes. "I didn't want to rehash those memories so I turned them down."

"What can I say?" Laynie shrugged. "Apparently, I'm going to be a best-selling author, just like you."

I couldn't blame her. Canusa Books could be very persuasive. 'Catching TCK' had been their biggest seller to date and they wanted to capitalize on my story while I was still news.

"I don't understand," Rhonda said.

"Behind Bars with the Black Swann," Laynie said, adding air quotation marks with her fingers. "It will be out some time in November, just in time for the Christmas market."

Laynie explained that she'd intended to ask for my help but had been both a little awe-struck and quite concerned about how I would receive her request given our history. She truly had been practicing her surveillance, while working up the nerve to meet with me face to face. Much to my surprise, it had taken Laynie less than an hour to convince me that after spending most of the two years we'd been in prison together plotting my demise, she no longer wished me harm. We were now on the same side, maybe future colleagues, with the possibility of becoming friends. With her ambitions channeled in a more positive direction Laynie was, dare I admit it, enjoyable and even quite charming.

Rhonda put away her phone. After a couple more stories, now certain I'd be okay alone with Laynie, Rhonda left and went to work. She took Betsy. I still had my bicycle chained nearby.

Laynie and I talked shop, continuing through a soup and sandwich lunch, until late in the afternoon. Her thirst for knowledge seemed unquenchable. We discussed topics ranging from interviewing suspects and witnesses, to handling yourself in dicey, even violent situations. She was very interested in my views on the balance between following your gut vs thorough investigating. I absolutely believe strongly that both are crucial to good investigation, as long as you don't allow your gut to overshadow or halt the search for the truth. Facts matter. Too often, as a detective, I'd witnessed other cops, most of them good cops, decide that a suspect was guilty and turn the focus of their entire investigation on that person allowing other evidence to go undiscovered or a trail to grow cold on the real perpetrator.

I learned that Laynie was miles ahead of me on the technology front. Apparently, she could hack her way into almost anywhere or anything, a skill she'd honed boosting high-end cars that were aluminum and leather-clad computers on wheels. My phone still got the better of me on most days.

I'd discovered that while Laynie hadn't gotten the huge advance that Canusa Books offered me for a second book, she'd managed to wrangle six figures after tantalizing them with a few details from our first fight in the showers. I was kind of impressed.

By the time the early bird dinner crowd was trickling in, it occurred to me that I was already mentoring my once sworn enemy. Her enthusiasm and thoughtful questions had won me over. I agreed to meet with her on a weekly basis, with a promise from Laynie that she would not do anything to violate her parole, including carrying weapons of any kind or stalking my friends or me. She promised. I kept her knife.

Was there room in the Okanagan for two private investigators? I guess we'd find out.

CHAPTER 20

By the time I rode home and got cleaned up, I only had a few minutes to reflect on the day's events before heading out to meet with my best friend. I realized that I hadn't gotten any work done on the Getz murder. I vowed to get back at it tomorrow.

Hannah was already seated when I arrived at the Whitespot on Main. She waved her arm as soon as I crossed the threshold. A pitcher of clear water, rather than frothy beer, sat in the center of the table in front of her, reminding me of my friend's new condition.

"I hope you don't mind," Hannah told me as I slid into the booth. "I'm famished, so I went ahead and ordered for both of us."

"Great, I'm starving myself." There wasn't anything on Whitespot's menu that I wouldn't eat. I was still trying to sort out the whole bazaar event that had just happened with Laynie and wasn't certain I could yet verbalize the story without sounding crazy. Besides, I was excited to tell Hannah about the Martins, Ross Gregory and the strange man in the videos. I led with that. "I have news about the Getz murder."

"Me too," Hannah said. "You go first."

"Alright," I agreed. "Last night I had a very interesting visit with Ross Gregory, the man who sold the vineyard to Milo. He suggested that the Martins next door..."

"I interviewed them," Hannah commented. "I thought they were a nice couple."

"So did I," I agreed. "However, they may have been harboring some resentment toward Milo. I think you and I should pay them a visit together and maybe apply some 'good cop/bad cop' pressure and see what pops out."

Hannah's phone rang. She looked at the caller ID. "Sorry, I need to get this."

"Of course."

"Hannah Buckley," she identified herself, and then listened for several seconds.

"Throw him into interrogation room one." She paused, listening again. Hannah looked at me and winked. "That's right, I want to let him stew for a little while."

It could be an effective technique, arresting someone and then leaving them alone in that quiet, bright room. Was there someone watching you through the two-way mirror? To all but the coolest customers, it could be quite intimidating. That simple piece of glass had elicited nearly as many confessions as good interrogators. To a guilty mind, minutes dragged by like hours. Poor schmuck.

"Just leave it all on my desk. Thanks Baker, that's great work. I'll be there as soon as I finish here." Hannah put the phone down and stared at me. I took the opportunity to continue.

"So what do you think, a little good cop/ bad cop action, for old time sake?"

"Won't be necessary," Hannah said, smiling.

"I thought you agreed that Milo's death seemed suspicious?" I asked. "What changed your mind?"

"Nothing much," Hannah said, glibly. "Except that we just arrested the man who killed Milo Getz."

"Ross Gregory," I offered.

"No," Hannah replied, then looked at me strangely, "why Mr. Gregory?"

"Just that he gave off some very strange vibes when I interviewed him."

"No, it was one: Guy La Roque of Nanaimo," she said. The name sounded vaguely familiar to me. "After I read several of the threatening letters he'd sent, I did some checking and discovered that La Roque had been sighted in the area several times in the past few weeks. I put out a BOLO and voila, he was picked up this morning on the highway to Vancouver."

The name sounded vaguely familiar, but I couldn't quite place where I knew it from. I'd been to Nanaimo a few times when I was a girl...

"And you have him here already?" I asked.

"High priority case. She reached into her purse, brought out a handful of folded papers and set them on the table.

"That man was at the party the night of the murder," I pointed out, recognizing the face in a photo on top of the pile.

"We know." Hannah nodded, then continued, "His daughter, Beatrice, took her own life and he blamed Getz for it."

"That sounds like motive," I commented. It sounded stronger than any motive I could think of that Terry Martin or Ross Gregory might have. Still I wasn't ready to concede yet.

"She was only fifteen."

"Oh no." Milo had had a reputation as a notorious womanizer before his marriage to Mavis, but I'd never heard stories about him chasing jailbait. "He and she hadn't..."

"No, it wasn't like that," Hannah assured me. "As far as I know Milo had never even met the girl."

"Whoa, you had me worried for a second." I breathed a sigh of relief for Mavis.

"She'd been teased mercilessly at school," Hannah said, rustling through the letters searching for a particular one.

"After Aurora released their album, Butterface had become Beatrice's nickname." She found the letter she'd been looking for. There was a Polaroid taped inside. She passed it to me.

The girl in the photo had a mouth full of braces, big glasses and was caught in that awkward phase where she was transitioning from girl to woman. "Poor thing." Some girls transformed gracefully during puberty, but for many like Beatrice, it could be a trying time. I recalled a couple of my friends from back in Junior High. I could see that maybe she'd never become a beauty-queen, but if she'd lived, she'd have been at least average looking. Kids could be cruel. She looked younger than fifteen to me.

Glancing through the letter, I could feel the anguish and pain of the grieving father. He blamed Milo squarely for the death of his wonderful daughter and promised egregious bodily harm if the singer's path ever crossed his own.

"Notice the date of the letter," Hannah said.

I looked in the upper left corner. "May 24th, 2011."

"And this one was sent May 24th, 2006." Hannah lifted the top letter and showed me the date, then picked up the next letter. "May 24th, 2015. They are all dated May 24th. I checked the records -- Beatrice killed herself on May 24th, 1999."

"That was twenty years ago," I said, doing the math.

"The big party at Butterface Wineries was on the 23rd. The coroner estimates that Milo's death occurred between 2am and 4am on the 24th. Coincidence, I don't think so."

"Probably not," I agreed.

"This letter arrived a few days before the party," Hannah said, moving it to the top of the pile. "It is the only one that wasn't sent on the anniversary of Beatrice's death."

The letter began by speaking of unbearable loss and how Milo could never understand how worthless his irresponsible music had made La Roque's daughter, and many other less than perfect looking young women around the globe, feel about themselves. As I continued down the page, the writing became erratic. I had to admit, Guy La Roque was looking like a very viable suspect.

"I did a full background check on our Mr. La Roque," Hannah told me, as she flipped open her notepad. "He was born on April 30th, 1972 in Chicoutimi, Quebec; played Junior 'B' hockey all over the country in the late eighties; got drafted by the Canucks in 1991, but spent most of his career bouncing around in the minors."

Hockey! That's where I knew the name from. La Roque hadn't been a star player like Gretzky or even Marcel Dion, but I'd heard the name. I tried to remember La Roque, the player. No images came to me, but I knew that I'd seen him play. Dad and I had watched many games together when I was a kid.

Hannah skimmed past a few details before continuing with the report. "Got married to an Yvonne Clement in Vancouver, in January of 1994. Beatrice, the La Roque's only child, was born a couple months later in March of that same year."

"For the next fifteen years he played sporadically for several different teams: Vancouver, Boston, Ottawa and Detroit. Then quit hockey in 1999."

"The same year Beatrice died." I pointed out. "Losing his only daughter had to be traumatic." I felt a deep sympathy for him and his former wife.

"It appears to have been life altering," Hannah agreed, looking up from her notes.

"Wait a second," I said, finally pulling an image of the hockey player from my memory, "he played for Ottawa in 1998. Guy La Roque had scored a short-handed goal that helped knock Toronto out of playoff contention that year." I'd watched that game with Trent. Trent had been a dyed-in-the-wool Maple Leafs fan, but I'd loved him anyway. Despite living in Toronto I'd stayed true to my beloved Canucks.

Hannah was about to say something, but our food had arrived.

"I've got a Monte Mushroom and a Bacon Cheddar," said a waitress, who'd materialized at the edge of our booth, carrying a platter with two massive burgers, sided with thick fries, on it.

"The Bacon Cheddar goes there," Hannah told her, indicating the space in front of me, while shuffling the papers off to the side of the table to make room for her plate, "and I'm the Monte Mushroom."

Hannah dug right in, but I wasn't as hungry as I'd been when I sat down. I took a couple of bites while I read more of the most recent letter. Beatrice had been a talented figure skater who dreamed of winning an Olympic gold medal someday. She'd been a straight 'A' student, until Aurora's hit album came out. It was clear that Guy La Roque believed that Milo's crass and irresponsible lyrics were directly responsible for his daughter's death. A sentence in the last paragraph was very telling to me. 'After reading about your winery and then seeing the labels with my own eyes, I believe that your phony condolences were empty gestures filled with hollow words.'

Seeing 'Butterface' all over again on the wine labels must have been horrible. I felt sympathy for the grieving father.

The last lines of the letter were: 'It is now clear to me that you have never truly felt pain in the charmed life you continue to live. You will, I promise you that.' It was signed 'Guy La Roque'.

"What's the matter?" Hannah asked, after swallowing the last of her burger.

"Nothing," I answered. "I'm sorry, this whole thing is just so sad, I've lost my appetite." She eyed my burger like a hungry hyena for a few seconds. "You can have it."

"No," she said reluctantly. "Thanks, though. I've already gained seven pounds and junior is only the size of a peanut."

"You've certainly got strong motive and means with this one," I told her.

"The guy is built like a tank," Hannah added. "He could easily have lifted Milo into that vat."

"Plus, he was at the party that night," I pointed out.

"Opportunity," Hannah agreed.

"Sounds like you've got everything you need."

"There's more," Hannah answered, as she popped the last of her fries into her mouth, all the while smiling like a Cheshire cat. "Did I mention what Mr. La Roque does for a living now?"

I shook my head.

"He's got his own demolition company," Hannah told me, glancing at my plate of food again. "Guess what a thorough search of the Butterface property turned up?"

I shrugged.

"Dynamite."

"Dynamite?"

"That's right," Hannah answered. "Under the southwest corner of the tasting building."

Though Butterface Wineries had that impressive gate and front wall, it didn't surround the whole property. In fact, the only thing separating Butterface and the Martin's vineyard was a shallow ravine. Anyone with a strong enough desire could get in. La Roque had such a desire – the anniversary of his daughter's death.

"Fingerprints, DNA?" I asked.

"Affirmative for fingerprints, still waiting for DNA."

"Nice work." I spilled my fries onto her empty plate. "Here, you've earned them, Detective Buckley."

As I worked on the back half of my burger, I suddenly remembered the unlikely playoff goal La Roque had scored. I remember the team spilling off the bench and piling on top of him.

I felt some sympathy for La Roque and the overwhelming grief that had caused him to cross the line and become a killer.

CHAPTER 21

Hannah invited me to come back to the station and witness her interview with the suspect. Though not as much fun as good cop/bad cop would have been, I accepted. I was happy that La Roque was waiting for us in Interrogation rather than in one of the holding cells. All those metal bars and the raw concrete could still get to me.

A uniform came racing toward us the moment we stepped through the precinct door. Pete Baker was fresh out of the academy; I'd met him a few weeks earlier.

"Hi Reggie," the keen rookie said to me before turning his full attention to Hannah. "The Unsub is in Interrogation One, just like you asked, Chief Inspector Buckley."

"He's not an Unsub, Baker," Hannah corrected. "Unsub stands for 'unknown subject'. We know who this man is and, besides, this isn't an episode of Criminal Minds."

"Oh yeah," Baker said, sheepishly. "What should I call him? The suspect or maybe POI?"

POI stands for person of interest. I had to admire Baker's enthusiasm.

"How about La Roque?" Hannah said.

"Well, La Roque is in Interrogation One," Baker announced.

"That's better." Hannah nodded approval. "Thank you, Inspector Baker."

"Probie," a harsh voice cut through the air from across the room, "if you're done kissing Buckley's ass, we've got our own work to do."

Inspector Vance stared venomously at Hannah for a couple of long seconds, then turned on his heels and stomped out. There was no love lost between former homicide detective Vance and current homicide detective Buckley. He'd tried to take the credit for the TransCanada Killer arrest from Hannah and ended up getting busted down to beat cop instead. Hannah's subsequent fame and fortune had been salt in his wounds.

"Good luck, Pete," Hannah called out to Baker, as he rushed away toward his partner.

My first look at La Roque was through the two-way. Big and burly were the first descriptive words that came to mind. The wide shoulders and crooked nose confirmed that the man had been an enforcer for the hockey teams he'd played on. Sitting there calmly staring straight ahead, he dwarfed the chair beneath him.

"That's a big one," Hannah said.

"Perhaps I should join you in there," I suggested.

"That's not a bad idea," Hannah said, then smiled. "Maybe we can get a little GCBC action, after all."

"Any chance I can be the bad cop this time?" I asked, already knowing the answer.

"Hah," Hannah snorted, shaking her head and rolling her eyes. "Give me a second, I need to grab something from my desk."

I returned my attention back to La Roque. His hands were palm down on the table. His eyes forward, unmoving, unblinking. The look on his face was not one of worry -- if anything, he looked at peace. I knew that he'd been in there for over an hour already. Interrogation rooms are usually a few degrees above room temperature, but you couldn't tell by looking at La Roque. This man was one of the cool ones. I wondered what thoughts were going through that oversized head.

"Ready," Hannah said, appearing at the Interrogation room door.

I nodded and joined her as she opened it and stepped inside. La Roque didn't flinch or acknowledge our arrival.

Hannah indicated that I should sit in the chair opposite him. She wanted to stand. Only when I moved into his field of vision did his eyes move. They locked onto mine. Dark brown, they were intense.

"Good evening, Mr. La Roque," I said, casually. "I'm Reggie Swann, a consultant with the PPD, and this is Inspector Hannah Buckley." Hannah grunted softly at the mention of her name. She was already pacing behind me. La Roque's eyes never left mine. "Do you mind if I call you Guy?" I took a chance on the pronunciation using the French version.

"Enough with the small talk." His deep voice betrayed the barest hint of his Quebec roots. "I know why I'm here."

"Good, that suits me just fine," Hannah's angry voice filled the room. "Tell us why you murdered Milo Getz and we can move you to a nice comfy cell."

"I'm not sorry he's dead, but I never laid a hand on the man," La Roque said, his eyes slowly drifting to Hannah and then back to mine. I didn't detect any signs of deception. I'd seen some very good liars though. We could be dealing with a psychopath.

"Where were you the night of May 24th, Guy?" I asked, watching him carefully.

"I was out," he said.

"With friends?" I asked, keeping my voice friendly. "Perhaps one of them could vouch for your whereabouts?"

"I was out alone."

"Maybe you were at the Butterface Winery party?" Hannah accused.

I knew he had been at the party from the surveillance tapes. I waited for his denial. If he lied this time with no indicators, that would tell me a lot about him, too.

"As a matter of fact, I did briefly attend their fancy party," he replied, his eyes steady, his voice smooth and even.

"A hah!" Hannah blasted from right above my head, startling me but causing no reaction from La Roque.

"I left hours before the party ended," he said.

"Where were you between the hours of eleven pm and two am?" she asked.

"Out for a walk." He glared at Hannah.

"Did your walk happen to take you onto the Getz property?" I asked.

"Yes."

"You killed him," Hannah lashed out. "I knew it."

"I already told you that I didn't," he reminded her.

"What were these for then?" she asked, producing two sticks of dynamite from behind her back, and then slapping them down on the table, a little harder than necessary for my comfort. La Roque didn't flinch. "We found them under the front seat of your truck."

"I'm a contractor," he shrugged his shoulders. "I have a demolition license."

Hannah stormed around the table and got in his face.

"You expect me to believe that it was just some big coincidence that Milo Getz was murdered on the anniversary of your daughter's death?"

The huge man's eyes bulged at the mention of his daughter. That statement had gotten a reaction. His hands clenched into meaty fists. I stood, readying myself to jump in and pull the brute off Hannah. La Roque's next move was unexpected.

His chin hit his chest and he said something that the noise from my chair legs scraping on the floor covered up.

"What did you say?" I asked, as Hannah backed away.

"Karma, it was karma," La Roque's eyes filled with tears. His shoulders heaved, and he began to sob.

"Are you admitting that you killed Milo Getz?" Hannah asked.

"I did not go there that night to kill him."

"But you did kill him, didn't you?" Hannah hounded.

La Roque stared at her, wiping away the tears with his flannel sleeve. Several long seconds passed. It looked like the man was finished talking.

"Perhaps it was an accident," I offered. "You confronted Milo and things got out of hand. It could have happened to anyone."

La Roque, looked at me as though I'd been speaking a foreign language. He opened his mouth to speak, then closed it and shook his head slightly. His eyes dropped to the table and he went motionless. La Roque drifted into the zen-like state he'd been in when we first entered the room. We'd lost him.

I glanced up at Hannah and shrugged.

She wasn't ready to give up on getting a confession just yet. Detective Buckley pointed at the sticks of dynamite. "We found more like these all over the Getz property. Your fingerprints are all over them."

La Roque didn't move. Though I could see tears forming in his eyes again.

"It's all right, you can tell us what happened." I pulled a tissue out of my pocket and set it onto his nearest hand.

He didn't react for several seconds. I was beginning to think we wouldn't get anything useful out of him tonight. A confession would be icing on the cake, but it probably wasn't necessary at this point anyway. Even Hannah appeared ready to call it a night. Then he surprised us.

"I just wanted him to feel even a small percentage of the pain I've felt every day since Beatrice left us," La Roque whispered.

"I am very sorry for your loss," I said, feeling his grief.

"I never meant to physically hurt anyone," he said, then lifted the tissue to his eyes.

Here comes the confession. Hannah was behind La Roque. She glanced up at the cameras in the corners confirming they were on. She looked excited.

"I was there, hiding in the fields," he said. "I was going to destroy his precious winery. That's what the explosives were for."

I glanced at the red sticks on the table. Dynamite, TNT, I tried to remember the difference. One was invented by Alfred Nobel and was more stable than the other. I couldn't remember which. They looked exactly like the one I'd seen in movies and roadrunner cartoons, except these fuses didn't look nearly as long. I felt a little uncomfortable being this close. Wyle E. Coyote never fared well when he was around the stuff. I had fewer lives to play with than the cartoon character.

"I was waiting for the party to finish," he continued. "I'd planned to do it just before midnight for Beatrice. By eleven pm most of the guests had left, but then Getz and two other guys went down to the barn. I didn't get a very good look at them from where I was hiding, but I recognized Getz's voice."

"That would have been Terry Martin, Milo's neighbor, and Ross Gregory, the former owner of Butterface Winery," I said, for Hannah's benefit.

"They were in there together for about half an hour, then they closed up and headed back towards the house."

"Did they leave the barn lights on?" Hannah asked, abandoning her 'bad cop' voice.

"Not that time."

"What do you mean, not that time?" I asked.

"The two guys left first..." La Roque began.

"Together?" I interrupted.

"Yes, together," he confirmed. "They walked to the front of the property, got into a car and left. Milo followed about a minute later after shutting out the lights and locking the place up."

Martin and Gregory leaving together matched the story both had told me during my interviews with them.

"You're sure he locked up?" Hannah asked.

"I know he did, because I tried the door a few minutes later."

"What happened then?" Hannah asked. I could hear some impatience creeping into her voice.

186

"I was setting charges around the tasting building," La Roque admitted, his eyes glancing from mine to the dynamite and then to Hannah's, "when I spotted a dark figure coming across the field. I watched it zigzag its way to the barn and slip inside a back door. A faint light went on in the barn, like someone using a flashlight."

"A dark figure? Really?" Hannah scoffed.

"Did he come across the field from the north or the south?" I asked, knowing that the Martin's vineyard was to the south.

"The south," he confirmed, then continued his story. "I finished setting the charge I'd been working on and was about head over to the barn when Getz comes waltzing across the yard."

Behind me, Hannah whispered, "Opportunity." La Roque stopped talking and stared up at her blankly.

"Who would Milo be meeting with at that hour?" I pondered aloud.

"It wasn't a planned meeting," La Roque stated, returning his gaze to me.

"Why do you say that?" I asked.

"Getz was grumbling about leaving a damn light on as he went past me."

"He must have been close by for you to hear that?" Hannah prodded.

La Roque squinted up at Hannah, then nodded.

"You could see him, but he didn't see you?" Hannah questioned, obviously not buying into the story.

"As soon as I heard him coming, I flattened myself onto the ground," La Roque explained. "Besides, he never once glanced my way, his attention was focused on the light coming from the barn."

"You have an answer for everything, don't you?" Hannah accused.

"What happened next?" I asked quickly to keep him talking.

"The moment Getz unlocked the door and stepped inside the light went out. A few moments later Getz yelled, 'Who's there?'

and then turned all the lights on. Then I heard some shouting. A heated discussion followed."

"Could you hear what they were arguing about?" I asked.

"I could make out some of the yelling," he told us. "Getz said something like: 'Damn it man, you scared the shit out of me' and I think the other man said: 'I had to know something, something'. I couldn't make out the last couple words. Then they argued back and forth for a few minutes, but I couldn't hear what they were saying from where I was."

Hannah let out a humph, conveying her disbelief. I however, still had not picked up any signs of deception. Either the man was an exceptional liar, or he was telling the truth. I was beginning to believe the latter.

Had Terry Martin forgotten something in the barn and come back across the fields at night to get it? What couldn't wait until morning? He'd definitely left that part out when I'd interviewed him. Perhaps Ross Gregory had been right about the grudge Martin held toward Milo. *How had I misread Terry Martin so badly during my interview with him and his wife?*

"You're sure they were arguing," Hannah pressed, to keep the big fellow talking.

"From the tone of their voices, yeah, I'm pretty sure they were arguing."

"Then what happened?" I asked.

"I didn't hear anything for a while," La Roque said. "I got curious, so I crept over to the window by the door. I thought they might be fighting."

"What did you see?" I urged.

"Nothing at first, I couldn't see them at all," La Roque shrugged. "But then I heard laughter."

"Get your story straight, La Roque. Were they fighting or having a party?" Hannah barked, pacing behind me once again.

"I know, it doesn't make sense, but that's what I heard," La Roque insisted.

"But you couldn't see them?" I asked.

"Once I heard them and knew approximately where they were, I spotted Getz. He was siphoning some wine from one of those big wooden barrels."

I recalled Roman saying that the oak barrels contained the new wine.

"Not from one of the big metal tanks?" I asked, to be certain. Terry Martin hadn't mentioned getting to taste the soon-to-be-released Pinot Noir. A lie of omission. I was still having trouble seeing him as a murderer. He'd fooled me completely.

"No, definitely from the big wooden barrels behind the tanks."

"What happened next?" Hannah pushed, not giving him time to think.

"Then he took the wine and two glasses over to a table by the far wall."

"What about the other man? What did he look like?" Hannah asked.

"I could tell he was at the table, but I couldn't quite see him from that angle."

"Come on, you couldn't see him, but you know he was there," Hannah laughed derisively.

"I knew he was there because Getz was conversing with someone. I saw the other guy's hand once when they clinked their glasses together, but I couldn't see the rest of him, honest."

"This is quite a story you've concocted La Roque," Hannah said, now leaning casually against the back wall. "Unfortunately, I'm not buying it. You were there, you had more than enough motive. I think Getz caught you in the barn that night, confronted you and things got out of hand. Maybe you didn't mean to kill him, but you did and then you covered it up – tried to make it look like an accident."

"That's not what happened, I swear." La Roque's pleading eyes swiveled from Hannah's to mine and back. I still could not see any signs of deception.

"Hannah." I nodded toward the door. "I need to talk to you for a second." I followed her out of interrogation. "I'm pretty certain he's telling the truth."

"A mysterious figure?" she replied. "I don't buy it."

"It could have been Terry Martin," I said. "He lives just across that field and he may have a motive."

"Not dead daughter motive. Besides, did you see those shoulders?" Hannah shook her head. "That man could have lifted Milo into that tank with one hand. There is too much evidence; I have to charge him. The courts will have to sort this out."

"Give me a couple more minutes with him first," I asked.

Hannah rolled her eyes and then opened the door.

"I believe you, Guy," I assured him, as I sat. "Tell me what happened next."

"I couldn't hear what they were saying, but Getz was all smiles now." An angry sneer curled the corners of Guy's lips down.

"That must have made you angry, on the tenth anniversary of your daughter's death, Getz is in there enjoying himself while your baby is laying in the cold ground," Hannah gloated, behind me.

La Roque balled his hands into huge fists. His knuckles blanched. "I wanted to march in there and tear that smile off his face."

"That's exactly what you did, isn't it," Hannah forcefully asserted.

"You wanted to, but you didn't," I countered. "Why?"

"I made a promise," La Roque whispered. He closed his eyes.

"What kind of a promise?" I asked, laying my hand on the closest fist.

"When Beatrice was eight years old, she found a video clip on line of me fighting with another player during one of my games. Things got a little bloody and it scared her. I told her that it was just a part of the game of hockey. She made me promise that I'd never hit anybody if I wasn't playing hockey. I made that promise and I've kept it."

I felt his hand relax.

There was a light knock on the door, before it opened. Annabel, the Crime Scene tech, poked her face into the room. Her eyes searched until they found Hannah's. Hannah nodded, then glanced at me raising her eyebrows. I could see she was silently asking if I'd be alright alone with the suspect for a few moments. I smiled assuring her that I felt safe. She slipped out of the room.

La Roque pulled his hand out from under mine. His face hardened again.

"What did you see next?"

"Getz got up from the table and disappeared from my sight for a maybe a minute. When he reappeared he was carrying an empty bottle. He looked over in my direction. I thought he might have caught a glimpse of me in the window. I ducked and hightailed it back to my hiding spot. Got there just in time, too. Getz came to the window, looked around, then shrugged and walked away."

"Did you ever go back to the window?" I asked.

"I stayed in my hiding spot for about fifteen maybe twenty minutes," La Roque told me. "It could have been longer. I was having second thoughts about blowing the place up. I'd looked at my watch. It was past midnight. I started thinking about my sweet little Beatrice. I felt like she was looking down on me at that moment. Down at her father, hiding in the bushes like the criminal I was about to become. I was ashamed. I knew she wouldn't approve. I knew at that moment I couldn't go through with it."

Maybe I'm a sap, but I believed his story. "Did you hear anything while you were in the bushes?"

"No, nothing," La Roque said. "Things had been quiet for a while when I found the nerve to poke my head up again. There was no movement, so I crept back to the window."

"What did you see this time," I asked.

"A sign from God," La Roque said, as he made the classic catholic sign of the cross. "Maybe it was a sign from Beatrice."

"Guy, what did you see?" I asked, knowing the answer.

"I saw a pair of legs sticking out of one of those big tanks."

"What about the other man, did you ever get a look at him?"

"I did get a glimpse of someone as they were going out the back door," La Roque answered, with an odd shrug as if something didn't make sense.

From my memory of the barn, while I was at the crime scene, I knew you couldn't see the back door from the window. "So, you must have gone into the barn."

"Yes, my first instinct was to help the person stuck in the tank," La Roque answered.

"But you didn't help him, did you?"

"No." La Roque smiled. "I realized two things as I got near to the tank. First, the legs weren't moving, and second, they belonged to the 'Son-of-a-bitch' Getz."

"How did you know it was him?" I had to ask.

"The fancy boots and leather pants," La Roque stated. "I recognized them from the party. It was him alright."

"What happened next?"

"I got the hell out of there." La Roque declared. "I rushed around trying to gather up the dynamite and blasting caps. In my haste I guess I missed one set."

"The dynamite provides the police with some very compelling evidence against you."

"I realized it was missing the next morning while I was packing up," La Roque said, looking at peace again. "I tried to go back to Butterface the next morning, but there were cops everywhere. So, I left town."

"You should have gone to the cops and told them what you saw," I told him.

"They would never have believed me," La Roque laughed. "I don't believe it myself. It doesn't make any sense."

"Why is that?" I asked, confused by his attitude. "Who did you see?"

"Milo Getz was killed by a ghost," La Roque blurted, sounding more than just a little crazy. His eyes went blank, staring right through me as if I weren't there. I was stunned by his statement. I'd believed almost every word until he said 'ghost'.

At that moment, Hannah burst into the room followed by two very large uniformed officers. I recognized Doug Finson, he'd transferred here from Edmonton a little over a year ago, and Roy Munson, a rookie from here in Penticton. I'd gone to school with his mother's younger sister.

"I've heard enough of this fantasy. Guy La Roque, you are under arrest for the murder of Milo Getz," she stated, then nodded at the officers. "Take him to booking."

Doug and Roy lifted La Roque by the shoulders and escorted him out.

"What just happened?" I asked, alone in the interrogation room with Hannah.

"You mean, besides finding out the man is batshit crazy," Hannah chuckled, before continuing. "Annabel matched his finger prints to some found inside the barn. They were on the inside door handle, the light switches and on the ladder."

"La Roque turned the lights out as he left the barn," I said, stating the now obvious conclusion. I shook my head. I couldn't believe how off I'd been about La Roque. I'd believed him. Despite the mountain of evidence against him, part of me still did. Except, of course for the ghost part. I hadn't seen that coming, at all. Then again, if it wasn't La Roque – it had to be the mysterious figure that had crossed the field from the Martin's place. I had believed Terry Martin, too. I felt totally befuddled. Then when you added Laynie Garcia into the mix, it had been a strange day from start to finish. On top of everything else, I hadn't had time to move any of my stuff into the new place. I was ready for this day to be over.

Just before I left the station, Hannah promised that she and Danny would come over tomorrow morning and help me move. I thought about going to Alan's place, but decided I needed some alone time. Sharing a blender of Okanagan Bliss with Mom on the deck and one last night in my old room sounded good to me as I rocked Betsy off her stand and twisted the throttle.

CHAPTER 22

Danny slowly backed down the last couple of steps into the basement. I could see the muscles straining in his shoulders and neck.

"How is it I ended up on the bottom again?" He grunted, accusing my boyfriend of conspiracy. "I've got all the weight on this end."

"I'll take that end on the next one," Alan laughed, following at the other end of my six-drawer dresser.

"This was the last one," Danny complained, then glanced back at me with pleading eyes. "This is the last one, right?"

"That is the last of it," I assured Hannah's husband. There were a few things left in my closet, but I'd get them later. "I was going to empty those drawers, but you he-men said you'd take it like that."

"Piece of cake," Alan laughed again.

"Easy for you to say." Danny set his end of the dresser down as soon as Alan came off the final step. He rubbed his lower back. "I think I may have ruptured my spleen."

"Your spleen is in the front, Bozo," Alan teased.

"Not anymore," Danny countered, causing both Alan and me to laugh.

"Just ten more steps, Honey," Hannah called from the kitchen, "and you'll be lifting nothing heavier than beer and pizza for the rest of the day, I promise."

"Now that sounds like a plan." Danny bent down, lifted the dresser and continued backing towards the spare bedroom. I followed them.

"It goes under the window," I directed. "Back this way, a little. Good, right there is perfect."

"Congrats, by the way," Danny said, as he straightened up. "Last night my wife told me that you guys caught the guy who killed Milo Getz."

"Hannah did it all on her own," I corrected him. I still wasn't convinced La Roque had killed Milo, though there was certainly enough evidence to convict him. On Monday I planned to ask Erika to talk to Guy. She was the best lawyer in town and he'd need the best.

"That's not what I hear," Danny stated. "There wouldn't have been an investigation if you hadn't taken the case."

"Pizza's here," Hannah said, appearing in the doorway.

We settled in my living room. Two pizzas, a half dozen beers and a liter of Coke disappeared pretty quickly. I headed upstairs to raid Mom's kitchen -- it wouldn't be the last time, I was pretty certain. I came back down with two bottles of wine and a big jug of Mountain Dew for Hannah.

"This is pretty good," Alan commented on the wine as I poured a second glass for him.

"Not bad," I agreed, though it didn't compare to Butterface's new wine. Nothing in the valley did. I was sworn to secrecy so I couldn't even brag about being the one that came up with its name or that I was part of a very small group of people who had tasted it and knew just how good it was.

I was halfway to sitting into my chair when I froze. Ross Gregory also knew how good the new wine was. Yet, Terry Martin told me that Milo hadn't relented to Gregory's pleas for a sample of it, the night he died. So how did he know? Gregory told me that his wine was once the best the valley had ever produced. Everything started to click into place.

La Roque had said he'd seen a ghost leaving the barn that night. I recalled just how much the winery owner resembled Frank Sinatra. Ross Gregory, former owner, knew those fields between the two wineries as well as Terry Martin. He must have dropped his former neighbor off that night and then crept across field to the barn. Milo caught Ross Gregory stealing or trying to steal a sample. The yelling followed by laughter suggested the intruder was someone Milo knew well. Ross Gregory also had motive. Jealousy over the wine or his estranged wife? Maybe both. I didn't have every detail completely figured out, but one thing I knew in my gut: Ross Gregory murdered Milo Getz.

"Are you okay?" Hannah asked, bringing me back to the present.

"Got your badge and gun with you?" I asked.

I was relieved to know that my spidey senses had been right all along. Neither Guy La Roque nor Terry Martin had lied to me.

CHAPTER 23

The house was dark when we pulled into the Gregory Estate Winery, but there were lights at the tasting room. Hannah drove directly there. Through the windows I could see Mr. Gregory sitting on a stool at the far end of the bar, near the trophy case.

Sinatra was singing 'It had to be you' as we stepped through the door. A soft bell rang announcing our arrival, though Gregory gave no sign of noticing. His back was to us, and we could only see one of his hands. Hannah drew her revolver, we separated and approached slowly. I could see two wine bottles in front of him – one empty with no label and I recognized the other as his prize-winning Malbec, which was almost empty. I relaxed a little once I was abreast of the man and could see he had a pen, not a weapon, in his hidden hand. I signaled for Hannah to remain where she was.

"Mr. Gregory, are you all right?" I asked, easing into his view. His red rimmed eyes slowly raised to meet mine. It took a few seconds before they registered any recognition of who I was.

"My last customer informed me that someone had been arrested for Milo's murder," he said.

"That's right," I confirmed, as I slid onto a stool a couple down from his. Nearby, yet out of his reach. "But we both know that he didn't do it."

Gregory nodded slowly.

"I was planning to, um," he paused and looked down at his hands. "I couldn't let another man go to prison for something I did. I planned to turn myself in once I was finished here."

"What happened that night?" I asked, moving to a stool next to his. "Why did you go back after the party?"

"I've regretted selling my winery to that man every day for the past ten years," Gregory told me, shaking his head slowly. "I had such plans. The Malbec was just to be the first of many award winners. But he offered me so much money. We had a lot of debt at the time. My wife convinced me to sell. We could buy another place and have a lot of money left over. I like it here, but those benches across the lake will always be closest to my heart. I was thrilled when I found out that Butterface was finally going to offer some fine wines. I tried to convince Milo to let me try the new wine, but he refused."

"You gave Terry Martin a ride home the night of the party," I said, trying to nudge him back on track.

"Yes, that's right," Gregory stated. "I knew that the building with the new wine inside was sitting there just across the field from his place. I pulled over at the end of Terry's driveway and hiked over. I'd slipped away to the back door of the barn and unlocked it earlier while the three of us were there. I let myself in and was searching for a small container when I heard someone enter the front door. I turned off my flashlight, but it was too late. Milo started yelling until he saw it was me."

"That's when you killed him," Hannah spoke for the first time.

200

"No, we argued for a couple minutes then Milo started laughing." Gregory smiled to himself, then at me. "He thought it was hilarious that I was so obsessed with the new wine. He said my crazy efforts had earned me a glass of it. He disappeared into the back and re-emerged a few minutes later with a tray holding two stemless glasses and a half carafe of wine. He led me over to one of the tasting tables. He put the glasses onto the table and set aside the tray. From under his arm he produced an empty bottle and set it down, as well. The bottle was larger than normal. 'Bigger is better' he chuckled, raising his glass in a toast. I raised my glass to his." His eyes closed as he remembered the details. "I gave it a swirl and could see that it had great legs."

"We're not here about the wine," Hannah interrupted. I hadn't realized she'd moved closer. I held up my hand to her indicating to let him talk. And he continued as if she hadn't spoken.

"I held it to my nose. The bouquet was exquisite. Then I took a taste..." His eyes opened, and he stared into mine. The intensity was startling.

"I couldn't believe it," he continued. "The Pinot tasted better than I even imagined it could. It blew my Malbec out of the water. I'd just tasted perhaps the finest wine ever produced in this country."

I remembered my first taste. I couldn't argue that point.

"So, you were jealous?" Hannah asked impatiently.

Gregory finally blinked and got a confused look on his face. He looked at Hannah like she'd spoken a language he didn't understand.

"That wasn't it, was it?" I asked, realizing I'd also been wrong about the motive.

"No, I was like a proud father. That my fields could produce a wine such as this made my heart swell."

"What happened next?"

"Then he told me that he'd just come up with a name for his new wine," Gregory looked down at the empty bottle on the table. "Maximum Pleasure."

"That's the name of Aurora's fourth album," I pointed out.

"I didn't know that," Gregory admitted, continuing to stare at the bottle.

"So you didn't like the name?" Hannah pressed him for more details.

"I thought it was an odd name, but better than his other wines," Gregory answered her, his eyes unmoving. "Then he pointed at the new bottle, told me that it was eight hundred milliliters instead of the standard seven fifty and handed me this." He stuffed his hand in his pants pocket. Hannah raised her revolver again, but she lowered it when a piece of paper emerged. He unfolded it and set the hand drawn label onto the bar between us.

From the precise penmanship I could see that Milo had been quite artistic.

Butterface Winery

Maximum
Satisfaction
Our Pinot is
bigger than theirs!

"That Pinot Noir is one of best produced anywhere and he was about to turn it into a phallic joke. The idea enraged me," Gregory continued. "The next thing I knew, he was on the floor and I was standing over him with the bottle in my hand. I didn't mean to do it. I don't even remember hitting him."

"Do you mind?" I pointed at the pen in his hand. I could tell, the repentant man wasn't a threat to either of us. I nodded at Hannah who remained alert, just the same. I reached across the table and took the offered writing instrument from him.

I stuck the pen into the neck of the bottle and carefully turned it over. On the bottom was a large smudge and tiny pieces of what I imagined was dried scalp. I held it outward for Hannah to see.

202

"Why stuff him into one of the tanks?" Hannah asked.

"I thought he was dead," Gregory told us. "I was panicking. Then I remembered how once a tank hatch fell on my head and darn near knocked me out. So, I hauled him up and hung him over the edge of the opening as if that had happened to him."

"You said you thought he was dead," Hannah prompted.

"I was about to shove him all the way in, when he started to sputter and kick." Gregory closed his eyes for a few seconds remembering that moment. His face masked with regret when he opened them and continued. "I almost pulled him back out." Silence filled the large room.

"Why didn't you?" Hannah asked, her voice just above a whisper.

"Those stupid leather pants," he stated.

He glanced over at the picture of his wife staring adoringly at Milo.

"If he hadn't been wearing tight leather pants I might have." He paused, closing his eyes before continuing. "Instead, I held his legs up until they stopped moving."

Hannah cuffed Gregory and informed him of his rights.

"Would you mind giving that to my wife for me?" He pointed at the stationary he'd been writing on, when we'd arrived, as Hannah guided him toward the door.

I read the short message on the top sheet. 'Dearest Victoria, I'm so sorry. I hope someday you can forgive me for what I've done. Love, Ross'.

"I'm afraid this will be evidence, Mr. Gregory," I told him truthfully. "But I will tell her."

Using the top of the pen, I nudged the top sheet to the side. The sheet below began with 'To Whom it may concern,' underneath was an abbreviated version of the account of Milo's death as he'd just described. He'd signed and dated the bottom.

I realized that the note to his wife was also a suicide note. I slipped around to the other side of the bar and what I found was no surprise. Next to an open box of shells, stood a sawed-off shotgun leaning against the bar across from where we'd sat.

I'm certain that if we'd waited until morning to confront Mr. Gregory we'd have found his body instead.

Six weeks had gone passed since I'd given Mavis the truth about Milo's death. That had been a tough day. Today was going much better.

Earlier in the day I'd finally tracked down Jamaica John. He was living in a halfway house in Osoyoos. Erika was thrilled. I smiled at her and Alan from my lofty head table position at the unveiling of Butterface Winery's new 'Concert' Pinot Noir. It was an exclusive party for friends and fellow winemakers.

"The labels look fantastic," I told Mavis. Since I'd inspired the name, she'd insisted that I sit at the head table with her and the Angelos. Mavis had picked out six of her favorite pictures of Milo performing at concerts and used them for the label backgrounds.

"Thank you," she replied. "I think Milo would have approved."

"Without a doubt."

Milo Jr. gurgled loudly next to my left elbow.

"He and this Milo, as well," Michelle laughed, holding her three-week-old son. She waved her baby's tiny hand at his dad who was busy pouring wine and doing his best to try and fill his late partner's shoes. Roman seemed to be doing just fine. Better than fine, actually. He'd even come up with the advertising slogan: 'So much flavor we needed a larger bottle'.

Just a year and a half ago, I couldn't have imagined having a day like this.

I caught Alan's eye again and mouthed, "I love you."

CHAPTER 24

Kingston, Ontario

"**S**tay calm, Reggie," I whispered, trying to slow my heart which threatened to crack ribs from the inside.

I ran my fingers across the smooth leather seats of the Lincoln Town Car. This was definitely not a prisoner transfer vehicle. There were no shackles binding my wrists or ankles, yet I still felt the same sense of dread as the first time I'd approached the Kingston facility. Arriving at the front entry for the first time, the glass-faced two-story building looked like an ordinary office building, with manicured lawns and a huge Canadian flag waving gently in the light breeze. In my mind all I could see, though, were hardened-steel cell doors, razor wire and long unmonitored concrete-clad hallways that lay beyond this façade.

"Two hours." I reminded myself.

"What was that, Ms. Swann?" driver Dan asked, glancing in the rearview mirror. He was a pleasant fellow in his forties, who was very adept at recognizing when his fare wished to converse and when they preferred silence. We'd chatted for the first half of the two-hour ride from the Toronto airport Hyatt, where he'd picked me up at 9am, but when I'd gotten quiet, so had he.

"Sorry, Dan, just talking to myself," I answered. I looked down and realized I had subconsciously rolled my notebook into a tight cylinder. Old habits... There was no point in bringing a briefcase into the facility. It, like me, would have to undergo a thorough search. I needed to get through security quickly, before I lost my nerve. Mostly for this reason, I'd worn no jewelry, beltless slacks and a buttonless, pullover V-neck sweater. Also, I remembered how resentful I and the inmates had felt when women came to speak to us dressed to the nines, seemingly having come to the prison directly from the beauty salon.

"I think what you are doing is very thoughtful and very brave. And I promise to be right here waiting for you when you are ready to leave." Dan turned and winked at me, as the car came to a stop.

"Thank you, Dan," I said, then winked back.

By the time I'd taken in and slowly released a deep breath, he'd slipped around the car and opened my door. His hand reached in, I gratefully took it and stepped out of the car. I stood looking at the building for several seconds. I left my small clutch-purse in the car. I figured it would be much safer with the bonded driver than in a building filled with thieves and miscreants.

"Would you like me to escort you inside?" Dan asked.

"Thank you, but that won't be necessary," I replied, realizing I hadn't yet let go of his hand. "Sorry, I'm a little nervous. The last time someone dropped me off here, I ended up staying for over eight years."

"That won't happen this time," Dan assured me. "I'll be right here waiting for you."

"If I'm not back in two hours and one minute call in the National Guard."

"You can count on it," Dan laughed.

I'd barely gotten halfway up the walkway when the front door swung open. A man and a woman stepped out into the bright sunshine to greet me. Both were smiling. I recognized the woman immediately, Warden Clarke. She'd been tough, but fair. She'd personally approved my request to run the prison perimeter rather than on the track with the other inmates. She, on the other hand, hadn't allowed me to go to a memorial service for my father. I'd missed his funeral while recovering from a stabbing that had nearly killed me. I'd always wondered if she'd have let me attend the funeral if I'd been healthy. As I approached, she seemed smaller and less intimidating than I remembered.

"Miss Swann, it is wonderful to see you," Warden Clarke spoke before I'd finished crossing the gap between us. She looked exactly as I remembered, dressed in business attire, nothing splashy but always neatly tailored – feminine, but stopping short of being attractive. She was dwarfed by the rather large man in beside her.

"Joseph?" I suddenly recognized the man, wearing a regular navy suit. I'd never seen the guard without his uniform and cap. His smile broadened. He stepped forward, extending his hand as I arrived.

"It is Assistant Warden Zabrowski now." His eyes sparkled with pride. My hand disappeared into his huge palm.

"Congratulations, you deserve it," I said, genuinely. The promotion truly was well-deserved in my opinion. Joseph had been one of the best guards in the facility. No nonsense, fair and unbiased, I had always felt comfortable in his presence and that had not been the case with many of the guards, male or female. The fact that he'd been recognized and promoted spoke volumes for how well the facility was run.

"Welcome back, Miss Swann," he said, adding a slight nod acknowledging my compliment.

"We're thrilled and honored that you agreed to speak to the inmates," the warden added, stepping forward taking my hand next. Though we'd known each other for many years, it was the first time we'd touched. Her shake was firm and strong.

"Thank you, Ms. Clarke."

"Call me Sandra, please," she said, guiding me toward the entry. "I hope your flight and accommodations were satisfactory."

"Absolutely top notch, Sandra," I had to admit. Though I'd turned down the speaking honorarium, I believe they'd spent it on me anyway. First class flights, a very nice suite at the Hyatt, plus, the luxury car and driver. "You didn't have to go to all this trouble for me."

"It is no trouble, Reggie. May I call you Reggie?"

"Please do."

"We don't often get to showcase an alumnus with such a success story," Joseph added.

Alumnus? The word caught me by surprise. It made it sound as though I'd attended the Kingston Federal Institution of Higher

Learning. If I looked at my time here in those terms, I'd earned a Master's degree in survival, with minors in making spaghetti sauce and folding laundry. After four years in the laundry facility I could neatly fold a shirt in under three seconds and during my time spent in the kitchens, I'd watched Roberta Pomodoro prepare her famous spaghetti sauce so often I could almost replicate it. Somehow, even though we used all the same ingredients, hers always tasted slightly better. Perhaps, it was the Italian songs she sang while cooking. Her voice is better than mine, too.

"Joseph is absolutely correct," Sandra said. "Capturing a serial killer, breaking up a national sex ring, and now an international best seller... You are truly an inspiration to us all, Reggie Swann."

I didn't feel inspirational as we neared the entrance.

"Thank you," I managed to get out, through my suddenly dry mouth. Joseph opened the door. I pushed down the urge to turn and run, took a deep breath and stepped inside. Warden Clarke continued to speak, but I couldn't concentrate. A little while later I'd notice that the floors were brown marble and the walls very pale yellow, but at this moment I could only see grey.

"I'll leave you in Joseph's very capable hands," the warden's words managed to worm their way into my brain. I pursed my numb lips into something that I hoped resembled a smile and nodded. "I have a couple of things to attend to before your talk. The ladies are so excited to see you."

"I can hardly wait," I managed, though in reality I could not remember why I had ever thought this was good idea to come here. If I survived today, I was going to somehow get even with Laynie Garcia for putting this insane idea in my head.

"See you in a little while." Warden Clarke smiled, then turned and walked quickly off.

"This way, Miss Swann," Joseph said, indicating toward a sign above a door that read: TRANSITION AREA.

Since I had no jewelry or personal effects other than a notebook with me, I was taken to a room where a female guard (one I didn't recognize) did a relatively thorough pat down. Unlike my first visit, I didn't have to endure a cavity search or delousing shower. When I got my notebook back, the staples had been removed. I hadn't thought about the damage they could do in the wrong hands. I should have.

My picture was taken and within a minute I was presented with a photo ID card on a red ribbon lanyard that I was instructed to wear all times. I'd seen similar ones around the necks of entertainers and speakers during my stay.

Joseph was waiting for me as I exited the room. At the end of the last 'free' hallway was a heavy metal door. Desperate memories of my time on the other side of that door flooded back. It is almost impossible to explain life on that side.

Especially when there is little or no hope of ever leaving. I laughed dozens, perhaps even hundreds of times during my time over there, usually during a movie or a sitcom, but it was never the carefree laughter you experience amongst friends. There is a sadness, a desperation for happiness that seeps into every cell of your being.

For the first few years that I was locked up I thought it was worse for me, because I was innocent and didn't belong. However, I came to believe that the opposite was true. Knowing that you put yourself in this situation was worse. When my cell door closed at night, at least I had a clear conscience. I had not done this to myself.

Once Joseph opened the door, I was suddenly aware of the monumental difference between the marble floors on this side and the polished concrete beyond. Ten feet ahead was a barred gate and beyond that was my old home. Joseph didn't have a key for the gate. The fresh-faced guard in the small control room, off to our right, inspected my lanyard and nodded to Joseph before turning a key and pulling a lever that unlocked the gate. The door behind me had opened and closed quietly; the gate, however, clanked loudly as the locking mechanism released. I tried to stifle the shudder that ran down my spine. My loose-leaf notebook could not have been rolled tighter. Old habits.

As Joseph escorted me toward the theater, a pair of guards accompanied us. One of them ten paces ahead and one ten paces behind. We passed the cafeteria. The doors were open, but it was eerily empty. Then I heard the distinct sound of a rack of plastic dishes being loaded into the auto washer, a chore I'd performed at least a thousand times. During the day there was always someone working in the kitchen. The normalcy of that relaxed me just a little.

As we approached the theater from the back, I could hear the Warden speaking.

"In just a moment, our surprise guest will come to the stage. She is a bestselling author..."

I heard a loud voice yell out, "Unless she wrote Fifty Shades of Gray, I don't care." There was a smattering of laughter.

"No, it isn't E L James," Warden Clarke continued, once the audience quieted. "This author works with the police on occasion." This statement brought a cascade of booing. "Hold on, hold on, we had to keep our guest's name a secret for security reasons, but now that she is here, I can tell you that many of you know her."

Loud indistinct murmuring erupted from the crowd, followed by several shushes.

"Please join me in giving a warm welcome to a woman that used to work in our kitchen and laundry facility, our very own Miss Reggie Swann."

I don't know what I expected, but it wasn't the reception I received as I stepped forward onto the stage.

The place went nuts. The cheering and noise was overwhelming, but in a good way. Someone shouted, "Blackie, Blackie," and soon the whole room was chanting my prison name. It sounded like there were thousands of people in the large room, rather than a couple hundred. For a few minutes, I got a taste of what it was like to be Milo Getz or Alanis Morrissette. Though, all I'd really done to earn this applause was survive my time here.

At first glance, it was a just sea of indistinguishable faces, but then I started to recognize many of them. Roberta and Leanne from the kitchen, Wilma Mainfield – my cafeteria mate, Betty, Cheryl and Dorothy from the laundry, Marie and Jen from the cells on either side of mine and many others that had mostly avoided any association with me and several who had made their outright hatred of cops or specifically me known. A few still bore the scars of our battles. I had to admit it was quite weird to see all these people cheering for me.

When the chanting finally died, I unwound my baton and looked down at the many words of inspiration I'd slaved over for days. I looked back up at the expectant faces. I let the loose pages curl back into a tube. These women did not want to hear a bunch of platitudes, I know that I wouldn't have. I took in a deep breath and spoke from the heart.

"To be completely honest with you, I never wanted to step foot inside these walls again. I spent eight years, two months, fourteen days and seven hours in this place. For much of that time, I believed the only way I'd ever leave was inside a pine box. There are a million places we'd all rather be right now." I heard several people reply, 'you got that right, sister'. I relaxed. "I really only came back for one more plate of the world's best spaghetti." Another cheer rose from the group reaching a crescendo when Roberta Pomodoro stood, did a small curtsy and blew a kiss my way. At that moment I shared a comradery with this group of women I had never felt the whole time I'd been locked up with them.

"How did things go?" Driver Dan asked, as we pulled away.

"Surprisingly well," I admitted. In fact, I felt invigorated. The experience had been quite cathartic.

Words had poured from my mouth. I didn't know I had that much to say. The hour had flown by as I covered many of the lowlights, as well as, the highlights of my life. I'm not a joke teller, however, the room had filled with laughter as I explained my many dilemmas in the modern world, such as: picking out a yogurt from the dozens of choices at Safeway or and my struggles learning how to use a smart phone. One of the biggest laughs came when I admitted that the first man I'd dated since my release turned out to be a schizophrenic serial killer. Hopefully, I had provided some inspiration, as well. I'd shared how my time inside had made me far stronger mentally and physically. Life isn't always easy, but every woman in this facility has the inner strength to handle any problem to come their way, whether it be a deranged murderer who both loves you and wants to kill you or attempting to retrieve a voicemail message from your new phone.

Best of all, I had the official recipe for Roberta's spaghetti sauce, including the secret ingredient I hadn't known about, in my pocket. Life is good!

The End

ABOUT THE AUTHOR

Wayne Kerr was born and raised in Biggar (New York is big, but this is Biggar), Saskatchewan. Twenty years ago, along with his wife and daughter, he moved to the United States. They have recently returned, and now live in the beautiful Okanagan region of British Columbia. When not reading or writing murder mysteries, he is probably hiking, kayaking or playing tennis.

Thank you for reading this Wayne Kerr novel.

www.ingramcontent.com/pod-product-compliance
Lightning Source LLC
Chambersburg PA
CBHW020607180626
46810CB00007B/2685